Bluebirds *of* Happiness

A QUILTED STORY

Jean Crawford

WestBow
PRESS

Copyright © 2010 Jean Crawford

All rights reserved. No part of this book may be used or reproduced by
any means, graphic, electronic, or mechanical, including photocopying,
recording, taping or by any information storage retrieval system
without the written permission of the publisher except in the case
of brief quotations embodied in critical articles and reviews.

WestBow Press books may be ordered through booksellers or by contacting:

WestBow Press
A Division of Thomas Nelson
1663 Liberty Drive
Bloomington, IN 47403
www.westbowpress.com
1-(866) 928-1240

Because of the dynamic nature of the Internet, any Web addresses or links
contained in this book may have changed since publication and may no longer be
valid. The views expressed in this work are solely those of the author and do not
necessarily reflect the views of the publisher, and the publisher hereby disclaims
any responsibility for them.

ISBN: 978-1-4497-0092-8 (sc)
ISBN: 978-1-4497-0093-5 (e)

Library of Congress Control Number: 2010923545

Printed in the United States of America

WestBow Press rev. date: 03/23/2010

In Loving Memory of a dear friend, Kathryn "Kay" Ruiter who worked with me in the office, went with me on a trip to see Niagara Falls for the first time, was an avid reader, encouraged me in my writing, and visits back and forth from Illinois to Florida. Her children and grandchildren have been blessed with her Christian legacy along with her husband, Mike's Christian testimony.

Acknowledgments:

A special thanks to all my family and friends who encouraged me in this project. My husband, Jim was amazing in his continuous and unending support of my writing endeavors. My daughter, Nanci Crawford, proofread the manuscript and gave me many helpful ideas. My son, Jim and daughter-in-law, Toni, encouraged me along with my daughters and sons-in-law, Linda and Steve Dohl and Donna and Tim Bult. Thanks to my sister and brother-in-law, Louise and Louie Kraft who gave me ideas; also my sister-in-law and brother-in-law, Pearl and Fred Lockeman, who encouraged me with the marketing and selling of this latest book. Thanks to all my friends and relatives throughout the United States, Canada and Ireland who purchased books and supported me in writing. May God bless them all.

Marie felt deeply her parent's change of attitude this morning. They were usually very happy when traveling to London, as it was a special treat. Even Jim, the coachman, would join them, laughing and singing as they packed the carriage but this morning Jim was as quiet as her parents. She even tried singing a song they had made up for their trips to London. "We are going to London to see the Queen," and each of them usually added more words to the song. This time she sang it by herself and her parents didn't comment or add any more verses. Mother and she would do so many things together, more than her friends' mothers, so it kind of made up for not having a sister like most of her friends.

Her best friend, Margaret, had two sisters but when she went over to her home the little sisters were just a bother to Margaret. Marie just wished that she had sisters or even a brother but she knew that would not happen. Mother had talked to her about it. She said that God must want her to be the only one. They usually stayed overnight in London since their home in Wimbledon was a little too far for a day trip but this time Papa said they would probably come right back home even if he had to go all night to get there.

The horses would rest for at least eight hours as they took care of their errands. Marie was confused as Papa was driving his horses, Jupiter and Mars, to London. She knew that Papa's good friend, Joe Black was in Debtors Prison now and Marie didn't understand that either. Mr. Black always seemed to have money for everything in their family. Her best friend, Margaret Black was never wanting for anything. She felt sorry for Margaret but at least she and the rest of the family had not been locked up along with her dad like many other families were when the father was taken to jail. There were so many things she just did not understand such as why their coachman, Jim, did not drive them this time and why when they left he lingered, waving Goodbye as if they wouldn't see him for a long time. Jim had the horses hitched to the carriage when they came out but then he turned the reins over to Papa. In the past, the Coachman had always driven them to London or, for that matter, any other place they went. Jim was always at the reins.

This is the first time she remembered that they were going without him. Even on the Trips they took, he would also join in their singing and add verses that made her laugh so hard she would almost not be able to come in on another made up verse. She knew all the servants were let go at Joe Black's home and their home was closed up. Margaret and her mother, along with her two sisters and brother, were staying with Mrs. Black's parents. She didn't know why the King didn't do something about it. After all, they would not be able to pay their debts if they were sitting in prison and some of them had been in there for years. They were going at a good clip as Marie mused about these mysterious things happening in her life. Her life had been so peaceful with nothing to worry about before this happened to the Black family. They would probably arrive ahead of schedule at the pace Papa was urging the horses to go. She just hoped they didn't run into any mishaps.

Just then Marie saw a gaggle of geese crossing the road. She was terrified that they were going too fast to stop but Papa stopped in time to let them go across. She turned to her mother who was sitting beside her in the carriage. "I am so glad we could stop, Mother as they seem to take it for granted that everyone will stop. There are five white ones and three darker ones. They are holding their heads up so high as if they had a perfect right to be there." Mother barely glanced at them but said they were very pretty birds as she kept thinking of all their debts. She would be glad when the trip was over. Elizabeth knew this was dangerous going to London because they could be picked up on the same charge as Joe. They were as deep in debt as Joe Black. They didn't want Marie to know about it and wanted to still give her the standard of living which their ancestors had experienced for generations. She didn't know what would happen to them. She knew God answers prayers so she had been praying continually for their safety in getting to London as usual and not disappointing Marie.

They were soon arriving in London and Marie decided to ignore her parent's actions and to focus her attention to the new dress they would be ordering. Papa stopped in front of the dress shop where Mrs. Johnson lived. Elizabeth and Marie climbed out. With just a nod in their direction, John continued on to the jail to visit his friend. Marie thought this was probably why Papa was so silent all the way here. He was really upset over his friend's arrest. Mother seemed to leave her worries behind as soon as they stepped into the dressmaker's home. This is where all Mother's dresses had been made. Elizabeth wouldn't need any this time but she knew her daughter's dress would be very pretty when Mrs. Johnson made it up. It took a few hours to pick out just the right material and to get all the measurements Mrs. Johnson needed. In fact, Mrs. Johnson even made them a cup of tea and they had a lovely visit. It soon came to an end and Marie stepped outside to wait for Papa.

She was getting impatient waiting while her mother was finalizing the purchase of Marie's dress. She would be coming back for fittings, at least two of them before her coming out party. It was November of 1716 and she would be sixteen on her birthday of December 28. Marie was so excited to be in London. Her girlfriends would envy her this Trip from Wimbledon just as they envied every other shopping trip to London. Marie looked back at the dressmaker's home, wondering when her mother would get finished and come out. The material was certainly not what she would pick. She felt like a pauper who didn't have money enough to purchase the really nice silks Mrs. Johnson showed to them. Mother had steered her away from all the more expensive fabrics. It was really not like Mother to be so thrifty. Normally her mother would let her pick out exactly what she liked to wear but not today. She also hoped there would be time to see some other things in London. They could even drive around London and see the castle and other sights….that would maybe make up for this disappointing trip for her dress. If Papa would only hurry. He didn't need to spend that much time with Mr. Black. If not for the food brought by Papa or other friends, he would most certainly starve to death. She knew that but Marie was still tapping her foot impatiently on the cobblestone walk when her mother finally came out to join her. As soon as Mother came out, Marie looked down the road to see Papa coming with the carriage. She was embarrassed that Papa had to drive his own carriage. She just hoped no one was around that knew her. She wondered again why Papa didn't have the coachman drive them to London. Marie was somewhat worried about Papa because he didn't seem as patient with her and she sensed her parents were being very secretive. She hoped it wasn't serious. As Papa pulled up she decided she wouldn't complain about the dress. She knew it would be pretty anyway even if it was not her favorite color. All her relatives commented on her beauty. Her blue eyes would just sparkle when they praised her. She had just recently changed her hairstyle, from wearing it down to wearing it in a bun that nestled on her neck. She would have her maid fashion her hair up for the festivities coming up for her and all her friends. She could just imagine how beautiful her friends' dresses would be. Some of her friends had dressmakers right in their own homes. Of course, they had sisters and brothers who needed clothes made for them also.

As soon as Papa stopped with the carriage after he called "Whoa" to the horses, she climbed in and Papa climbed out to help Mother into the carriage. Marie noticed Papa's silence again even between her parents and he was even quieter when they started this trip. It was entirely different from any trip they had ever taken together. She knew how much her parents loved each other and how they were always showering her with gifts and love. Papa always said he was so proud of his daughter and it was no secret that she would inherit everything they owned.

They proceeded down Charing Cross Road. The silence was killing Marie and made her so nervous that she forgot all about her promise that she would not bother her parents about the fabric or the color of her new dress. Breaking the silence, she blurted out, "Mother, I thought we would have chosen the beautiful silk material. It would have looked so nice with my blue eyes." She continued, "I don't know what that brown material will look like on me with my black hair." Elizabeth looked lovingly at Marie. She wished she could buy her anything she wanted. How could she explain to Marie the financial bind they were in now?" It wasn't like Marie to be so unappreciative of their provision for her. She didn't know what she would say when they arrived home and all the servants had left. Elizabeth and John were both raised in a class of landowning people who were just below the nobility. They would have a hard time getting used to a home without servants taking care of their every need.

Elizabeth just hoped that Uncle Richard would be able to bond them out of this tragedy they faced. She knew John was beside himself with worry. There were so many creditors that could demand their money and turn him in. Elizabeth wondered about the friend who was sitting in the Tower of London prisons. She had sent some food with John but it would not do more than a couple meals. She tried to consol Marie. "You will look beautiful in that dress, Marie. We are having hard times and we will have to cut down on our purchases. We are doing the best we can for you, honey." Marie loved her parents and was sorry she had complained even after she had determined not to say anything.

Marie leaned back in her seat and decided to just enjoy the scenery. She would not bother her mother about the dress again. Anyway, maybe with the lace around the collar it would take the brown color away from her face They were almost out of the city of London when Marie heard the sound of horses' hoofs coming up behind them. Mother was sitting with her eyes closed. She looked so tired and was so startled when the policemen stopped by their carriage. "Whoa, Whoa," Papa said as he pulled on the reins. The horses stopped immediately and John faced the policeman who drew up beside the carriage first. "John Martin, We have a warrant for your arrest. Will you follow us back to London Towers, Please?" Ignoring Elizabeth's moaning and John's anger, he said," You can get everything settled there, Sir. We just are carrying out our orders for your arrest."

The family never arrived home and no matter what Papa said or how much he bargained with the authorities to let his wife and daughter free and just keep him, they were all put in jail. Papa was so distraught about his circumstances that he could not even carry on a conversation with Elizabeth and Marie after they were put in prison. All that Marie knew was that they were in debtor's prison. She had no hope that they would be released. She would not be at the party or wear a beautiful dress of any material. The clothes on their backs were all they had. There was no time given them to go home for extra clothing or anything else. They were in Debtor's prison or a dreadful Den and would have only the food and clothing their friends could bring them. Marie really didn't want anyone to see her like this and hoped her friends would not come with their parents to bring them anything. Their long, boring days went on and on. She could see her mother sorting through the food, trying to ration and save some for the next day. They were given water and some kind of watery gruel from the jailors. Their friends came by occasionally to supplement their food and to bring them some of their clothing. One day a Clergyman came by with a Bible for them. Mother started with Genesis and read to them every day. At first Marie didn't even want to listen to the Bible. After all God had forsaken them sending her family into a dungeon like this. But in desperation she joined Papa and Mother in their prayers to God, asking that He send someone to release them. The only joy she had was a yellow kitten that stayed by her side. His jailors allowed the kitty to stay because he kept down the mice and rat population. Some times she would hear a beautiful Irish voice singing praises to God. Marie remembered the day he arrived and as he passed by their cell she could see his lean form and his beautiful red hair. She didn't know why he was put in here but after two years of their jail time, it was wonderful to hear him sing. Sometimes the jailors would put a stop to his singing and told him to quiet down.

Finally, twelve years later in 1728 Colonel Oglethorpe was appointed to a Committee by Parliament to inquire into the condition of Debtors Prison in London Tower. And then one day

Marie heard James Oglethorpe coming down to their Cell. The other men appointed to this committee accompanied him.

They were all grieved about the condition of their friends in this terrible situation. Marie thought surely God had finally answered their prayers. Colonel Oglethorpe gave them hope when he told them of his plans for the men, women and children in such dire conditions. But Mother was so weak she could hardly lift her head. "I truly fear for my wife's life," Papa said as he appealed to the Colonel to include them in his plans to place The Debtors in the colony of Georgia. Colonel Oglethorpe also was resolved to bring the jailors to punishment.

Marie would never forget the day her Mother passed away soon after they talked to Colonel Oglethorpe. Her mother's last words were engraved in her heart. "God has answered our prayers. Marie, please don't be embittered by our situation. I am going home now, rejoicing in our Lord's protection all these trying years. Remember when we were reading Psalm 90:10 where it says our life is soon cut off and we will fly away? The real me….my spirit will fly away. May God bless you and keep you safe and John, be sure to enjoy your new home in America. Think of me in Heaven. I know you have been worried about where they put my body but it doesn't matter, dear. Remember my soul will be with Jesus. I will be waiting for you in Heaven" They had to lean close to hear her speak. Her voice had become weaker daily. Marie and Papa kissed her gently. They loved her so much. Papa had to beg the jailors to remove Mother's body from the cell for burial. At last a jailor came who had more compassion than the others did and sent one of the gravediggers to take care of her body.

Marie had covered her mother with the beautiful quilt her mother had made long ago. It was the Bluebird of Happiness Quilt. She didn't know if they would follow Papa's orders or not but at least he tried. They wanted her to have something of beauty around her as they put her mother in the grave. They knew there would be no coffin or Tombstone but she would be forever etched in their hearts as they thought of her love for them and her constantly denying herself of food until she saw that they had enough. They knew her soul went to heaven and they would see her again.

It was a bitter- sweet day when Colonel Oglethorpe returned with the keys to release them. He told them they would be going to Georgia on the ship, Anne. They only met the other prisoners as they were led out of the Tower. Marie recognized so many voices she heard all those years. It was great to put on the clothes the Colonel had given them. Their jail clothes were given back to the jailors. Soon they were all standing on the dock in their new clothes provided by Colonel Oglethorpe, awaiting the long voyage ahead of them but they were so grateful to be included in this journey as they looked forward to seeing America for the first time.

Chapter 1

The colony would be called Georgia in honor of King George II. It was cold on the dock waiting to board the ship Anne from Gravesend on this November day of 1732. Marie and Papa were so grateful to Colonel Oglethorpe for finally making it possible to release them from bondage. Their only heartache was that Mother would not be with them as they took this journey to the colony of Georgia but then they remembered what Mother had said just before she passed away. She wanted them to enjoy the new land and the new opportunities. It was important to her that they would be free. They knew God would see them through this journey to a place where there would be new friends and new experiences.

Marie looked around her and she knew she recognized some of the voices. One young fellow seemed to stand out from the crowd. He was tall and had red hair. She knew that he was the one she heard singing especially in the early night hours as they were held in bondage. The singing had always helped her to fall asleep and along with her mother's encouragement it helped her to pray for their release. She had never dreamed that it would mean traveling to another country. What would she have done without her mother? She not only lost her mother but also her best friend. Mother was a friend to her the whole time they were jailed. As Papa was engrossed in the studying of the Bible, Mother would tell her all kinds of stories about growing up in Ireland.

Marie had lost track of her friend, Margaret. She was glad Margaret did not come with her mother to bring them food but that stopped too five years ago. She did hear that Mr. Black was released but after the settlement he was penniless. Marie hoped that Margaret had been able to marry in this time and establish her own home. Mother would tell Marie stories about her parents, which would be Marie's grandparents. Her grandparents lived in Ireland and Mother was sure the young fellow who was singing was Irish. His tenor voice had been appreciated by all until he was told by the jailors to quiet down.

It seemed everyone had moved down farther on the dock now especially around one older man who was standing next to Colonel Oglethorpe.

Marie nudged her papa, "Who is the man over by the edge of the dock, Papa? It looks like he has gathered some of the people around him to pray." Marie thought they should be praying too for this trip over the ocean. She looked at the ship in awe. The sailors were getting ready to unfurl the sails that would be a difficult task in light of the strong November wind.

John was so thankful Colonel Oglethorpe had the compassion to work for their release. He imagined it had not been easy to convince the King and the parliament. It was wonderful to see Marie in clean and proper clothing. The clothing must have come from Colonel Oglethorpe's friends. Marie's blue dress with the ruffles and lace trimming was very pretty on her and complimented her beautiful blue eyes. Her black hair was caught up in a bun. Papa was grateful for his clothes also. He knew they would not stand out in a crowd now but would look like the average persons—and not someone who had served time in Debtors Prison. Of course they were still very thin and looked pitiful. Hopefully that would change when they had some food to eat. Marie's dress was just hanging on her but she didn't care. She knew better days were coming when she could get enough to eat. This had been hard on Papa and in the daylight she could see his silver hair, which once had been a beautiful auburn.

John turned to his daughter, "Marie, we have been praying daily but we can go over there and pray with them if you wish. I believe that is Rev. Shubert standing beside Colonel Oglethorpe. He said something before about getting him to accompany us across the ocean. Papa looked at his daughter with love. He knew he couldn't dwell on the loss of his wife but must live for his daughter's sake. She had missed out on all the activities most young people participate in and he could see she was anxious to meet the other passengers.

"I think Colonel Oglethorpe is motioning to us to join them over there. It might be about time to board the ship," he said as they started walking towards the rest of the passengers. Marie would be glad when they could get out of this cool wind. Everyone said this ship was built on the order of the Mayflower. These would be their companions for the whole month and into December and maybe even into January. She was grateful for the warm clothing that Colonel Oglethorpe had given them. As they approached the crowd Colonel Oglethorpe welcomed them into the group. Everyone on the passenger list was now present and accounted for. After all of them were gathered together they bowed their heads and prayed with Rev. Shubert. Not all the passengers had been prisoners at the Tower of London. Some were going to try innovative farming methods in the new land and some were going for religious purposes. "Let us all bow our heads in prayer and thanksgiving for the promise of a better future for all of us," Rev. Shubert said as they all bowed their heads. "Heavenly Father, we come to you with thanksgiving in our hearts. We thank you for this ship and pray that you will keep us safe as we sail. We thank you for Colonel Oglethorpe. He has fought for two years for this vision to help us leave jail and start a new life.

May we receive comfort for the loss of our family members before he succeeded in convincing King George and the House of Commons to let us go. May we always acknowledge you, Dear Lord, as our King and our Lord. In Jesus name.....Amen." Marie held hands with Papa throughout the prayer and then dropped his hand as the others had started to line up to board the ship. Marie was sure the young man with red hair was the Irish singer and as they waited to board the ship she listened to his voice asking Colonel Oglethorpe questions about their trip to America. She also noticed some girls who looked about her age. This was like heaven to be with so many people after being isolated for half of her life. She was anxious to board the ship and to leave England forever. It still seemed too good to be true and she became frightened anytime she would see English military, thinking they were ready to take them back to jail. She would not rest easy until the ship sailed away from the coast.

As they joined the other passengers, Marie kept looking up at the large ship. It was so tall with all the sails. She wondered how they would ever get across the ocean in this very tall and large ship. She could see the sailors raising the sails. Each sailor seemed to know how to get the ship ready for sailing. John Martin and his daughter Marie were almost first in line. The ship was a three-masted ship. The sailors were still working with the sails. They seemed to be in good humor and anxious to make this trip carrying all the passengers. The sailors were young men interested in seeing the world as they worked for their passage and to support their families back in England.

Marie was excited but she noticed Papa was very quiet and knew his heart ached for his wife and their life he was about to leave behind…their life before they were taken to jail…their life with all their friends and relatives living in mansions they had inherited. John had always marveled at the way Elizabeth could soothe his spirits and made each day they spent in jail an encouragement to block off one more day closer to when they would be released. They would often talk about when they would be free and their sadness for Marie to spend half her young life in this terrible place. They would talk about when she was born and their wishes for the best education for their daughter and wishes for her to meet the right man, who would love her, as they loved each other. He hoped with a new beginning he could provide everything that Marie would need. Now they were boarding the ship. Their possessions, such as they were, already were down in the hold of the ship. They surmised they would all be sleeping below deck. Marie told Papa she was really frightened of the ocean but she knew she needed to trust the captain and the sailors to get them across this big ocean. She decided, as her mother would say in her Irish way, "she would change not a clout until May was out" so she would change not a clout until they reached the other side. She could just picture the ship going down and she would be in her nightclothes before everyone as they escaped. She decided she would just change her underclothes but never wear her night- clothes. Papa hoped the prayer of Rev. Shubert would help Marie to know they were in God's will and would be establishing a Christian home in Savannah, Georgia.

Everyone was on deck as the ship pulled away from the shore. There was a mixture of tears and laughter as the 35 families made up of 120 immigrants—men, women and children sailed from Gravesend for Georgia in the ship Anne, of 200 tons burden, on the 6th. Of November 1732. Marie was tearful as she thought about her mother and when she looked up at Papa he was smiling through his tears. When he was as young as his daughter he would have regretted leaving dear old England but the time at the jail in the London Towers cured him of ever wanting to come back. No place could be as bad as they had experienced the last sixteen years.

As he looked at the other passengers standing on the deck, he noticed the Irish young man with bowed head probably praying for a safe voyage as John did, "May it please God to bless us in this new land," he murmured as they continued on their way.

Chapter 2

Marie looked up at the white sails in awe as they started their journey. The land continued fading in the distance and as she looked up at Papa, she couldn't help but notice a difference in his attitude. He had become a man who was discouraged and humbled, especially after Mother had passed away. But looking back on him now and his proud stance she saw his hope for the future. He seemed to breathe a sigh of relief, as turning to his beautiful daughter, he said, "Marie, how often I have wished I could provide you a better life. I always took everything for granted….our beautiful home and all our servants, our horses, trips and our freedom. That has all been taken away from us and I am very sorry. We will start a new life. God has answered our prayers and left us with a promising future in a new land. Oh look, we can see the land of England receding from our view." As she tried to wrap her cloak around herself to keep warm, John noticed her shivering and decided he must get her shelter soon. He saw her hands were half frozen. Everyone seemed cold but they all had cloaks and hoods supplied by the Colonel. It would have been better if they had come last spring or summer but it took so long for King George to make up his mind to let them go. All the papers had to be signed and approved by parliament. Colonel Oglethorpe especially wanted to give these people a chance to make a living after a friend of his died in Fleet Debtor's prison when he contracted smallpox. They had stood in line a long time before they were allowed to come aboard the ship. Her black hair was shining in the winter sun and strands of it were blowing across her face. "I am so sorry you are so cold, Marie, but I think Colonel Oglethorpe is doing the best that he can to get us all taken care of. He told me our sleeping places will not be good but it was the only way he and the Captain could decide where everyone would have a good place to sleep.

"Papa, anything would be better than what we suffered in prison. I just pinch myself to know that we are out of that horrible place. I know all these people surrounding us had much of the same experience that we did. I just pray that God would bless our King and Colonel Oglethorpe for bringing this about for us. As Mother would say, 'God has something special for us.' I just regret she will not be able to share it but I know she is in a better place."

As John looked into her eyes, he saw so many similarities to his wife, Elizabeth. How he and Marie had depended on her faith. "Colonel Oglethorpe will find a place for us all to sleep, Marie. I know he will do his very best working with the Captain. This is already the sixth of November and he doesn't think we will arrive to our destination until sometime in January. The Captain of the ship has provided two places of privacy using the pieces of canvas he had on the ship."

They could see the Captain talking to the other passengers as he approached them. Marie did not remember the wind this strong before she was put in jail with her parents. "I will be glad to get out of this wind, Papa. My hair must be a mess. It will be so snarled I will never get a brush through it." As she looked around at the other passengers she noticed that a lot of them were going below the deck to get out of the wind.

"Let's just follow them down there, Papa. This is such a cold breeze. Even with this cloak, I am just freezing." The breeze was coming off the Atlantic Ocean and the wind was filling the ship's sails. They were off to a good start.

"We'll do that, Marie. I see you are still weak so hold onto me and we will find you a good place out of this wind. I guess there certainly is enough wind to fill those sails." Marie felt like her feet would slip from under her so she held John's arm as they proceeded to follow the other passengers. They saw more passengers who looked like skin and bones but Marie and John knew they didn't look much better their selves.

John knew that Marie would have more food to eat on the ship than she ever had in the jail. Food brought memories back of his wife dividing out the meals that were given to them and how he knew she didn't give herself as much as he and Marie had to eat. She only had enough to eat when a friend would come by with some food and at first they did bring food and even some clothing but that didn't last. At times they felt forsaken by their friends but except for Joe, they did not do any better themselves before they were put there. He just hoped Marie would be able to regain her health and strength. She stumbled a little on the first step but grasped Papa's arm and felt a hand behind her trying to help steady her. She looked back over her shoulder and found out it was the young man she had talked to before as they gathered to pray for their trip to America. "Thank you, Sir. I find myself so unsteady on my feet. I guess I will have to get used to sailing."

"You are very welcome, Miss," he replied. He looked funny with his red hair standing on end from the wind. She wished to get better acquainted with this young man. He looked to be in his 30's and probably about her age. The Captain of the ship stood at the bottom of the stairs handing out bags that were filled with straw or feathers to use for sleeping. Marie knew that the ladies interested in their plight had made them to keep them comfortable in their sea voyage to the New World.

As Marie looked around she wondered how everyone would fit during the night. After all, there were one hundred and twenty people consisting of men, women and children. Most of them were from the Debtors Prisons but some were just without work in England and King George II thought they would have a chance to earn a living in a new land. At the same time it would relieve their government of the expense of providing for them, such as it was. They would still be considered English citizens- even the babies that would be born in America. As Marie stepped down with the crowd, she was handed a large pillow to sleep on at night and one was given also to her papa. She didn't know the work that the ladies did as they made the pillows and stuffed them with straw and feathers,

John was pleased to see his daughter making friends with a lady he had seen before when they were all gathered for prayer. She looked like a nice girl so he was glad she had found someone so quickly. She would be safer with passengers her own age. He knew he would not be able to look after her at all times. He regretted the sixteen years his daughter had spent in Prison.

He wished he had been more careful in his business practices and hired the right people to work for him to oversee his financial records. John remembered how glad they were to be allowed to keep their Bible and could have interesting discussions and prayer to God, thanking him for their salvation and asking Him to send someone to help in their dire circumstances. He turned to the man next to him who introduced himself. "I am Ted Miller," he said putting out his hand in friendship. John could see this man would make the journey bearable with his friendship and interesting conversation. John had made a good observation for Ted proved to be a valuable and good friend for years to come.

"It is good to be able to talk to someone besides a jailor who has no interest in your welfare, John. I had friends coming to see me at first as I know you did also. I don't blame them but I am glad they brought some clothing and writing materials that we could use to pass the time."

"I am thankful to King George for listening to Colonel Oglethorpe and making a way for us to have a second chance. I have my daughter with me. Do you have anyone with you, Ted?"

Ted waved to a lady not far away from Marie. "That is my wife, Ruth, John. She has suffered so much through all this. We lost our baby daughter while in prison. The jailor just refused to get us any help and this took place after our friends had forsaken us. We had no way of communicating with them."

"I understand," John said. "We had the same trouble when my wife became sick. It was sad when we left with Elizabeth in her grave. How I wished this had happened before she died." John sat down on his bag of feathers and bowed his head. He decided he would never get himself in a situation that put him in jail again. He would see that he always paid his bills or work it out. He had never worked with his hands but he could learn anything. He would do anything to support his daughter and himself.

Ted was sorry for John. It must have been terrible to have a daughter with you in these circumstances. Colonel Oglethorpe had said they would have to learn new skills. This was a new land they were coming to and they would need farmers, carpenters and just so many jobs that these men were not prepared to do. The farmers would be given land to farm.

Colonel Oglethorpe was going around now and speaking to each of the one hundred people of his responsibility. He stopped to talk to John and Ted. "You can see men, that it would be impossible for all of us to sleep down here. The Captain has told me there are lots of hammocks on deck and the men will have to make do with them. There will be places of privacy both for the men and the women. He has marked off two areas with some canvases which he hopes will accommodate us for the journey."

Ted and John noticed the regal bearing of the Colonel. He was a man that would stand out in a crowd. He was a man of compassion, putting the welfare of others before his own needs. He was a man of patience, never giving up on getting the King's permission to establish this colony, especially after losing a dear friend in Debtors Prison. His kindness showed forth in the way that he greeted each person on board.

"By now, I guess you are all hungry but the cooks on board are making us our first meal as we talk," Colonel Oglethorpe said as he continued on through the crowd of people gathered together in this venture of colonization.

Marie joined her Papa now along with the girl she had befriended. "Papa, this is Alice Palmer and she was imprisoned with her parents also but they both died in there so she has come all alone to our new colony."

John could tell that Alice was a beautiful girl but so malnurtured that it would take a long time for her to regain her beauty.

She seemed to lack the energy to even care for her blond hair that was falling down her back in waves. This would be a good friend for Marie. "You are very welcome to stay near us, Alice. We would appreciate hearing your experience and your willingness to come over to a new land."

The ship Anne was progressing across the ocean as they talked and the smell of food cooking was seeping below deck where they were all gathered. They were wondering if the Captain expected them to come on deck to eat. Each person had their own eating utensils and bowls all made of pewter. Some had brought their own but Colonel Oglethorpe supplied the tableware to anyone who didn't have any. They heard the Captain's voice as they rang the dinner bell. "All hands on deck!" he said and immediately the sailors left the passengers and reported to the Captain.

The passengers all put their pillows down on the floor of the ship and waited for their meal. Everyone was hungry by now. John motioned to his daughter to join him as he saw other families gathering together. The sailors started coming with the food served in trenchers. All the food had been dried but was cooked to perfection for the passengers. There were biscuits and peas, which were carried on the ship dried so that they would have nourishing foods. They had cooked the dried fruits, which made a nice dessert. The ham was delicious and everyone had a small piece. The hold was silent as the passengers partook of a meal far superior to the ones they ate in jail or on the streets.

Marie smiled as she looked at Papa who had already finished his meal. "Oh, Papa, I can just picture Mother sitting here with us. She would have been so happy that we were getting enough to eat." John was so pleased that Marie finally could eat in peace and he just knew she would be healthy by the time they arrived in this new land. He had thanked the lord for the food before but now he bowed his head and thanked the Lord for giving them this opportunity. "Praise ye the Lord, O give thanks unto the Lord; for He is good and His mercy endureth forever." John knew their prayers had been answered and he knew now why this verse from Psalm 106:1 had given him comfort in jail. He knew that God had a special plan for him and his daughter. Alice and Marie gathered up their plates to go on deck to clean their pewter ware. They noticed the ocean and beautiful sunset as they went on deck.

"Look, Alice, we don't see the land anymore, just the ocean as far as we can see but look at the beautiful sunset." Marie couldn't get over how much she had missed being in jail all those years and never seeing the sunlight or the beautiful ocean. She saw them before they were thrown in jail and tried to picture those things in her mind while she was in jail but what she remembered did not compare to the real thing. She turned to Alice who was wiping away her tears.

"This must be like Heaven, Marie. Mother and Father talked about Heaven and how we would be so happy when we went there. I felt so deserted when they died and left me here on earth but, Oh, Marie, I am so glad I found you and I hope we will continue to be friends even after we reach the new land." Alice looked beautiful as she watched the ocean while she talked. Her blond hair was waving to her waist and you could see that her prison time had not made her bitter. Her sweet expression touched Marie's heart.

"I am so grateful for my parents and I can understand as you are talking that you had Christian parents too. I hope we can remain friends, Alice. We will try to see that we live close to you when we reach our new homes."

It was still very windy out on deck so the girls decided to get their places to sleep below deck. Marie hoped Papa would be able to find a place to hang his hammock out of the wind. As they went down the stairs, they could hear Rev. Shubert gathering them all together once again to ask God to keep them safe during the night. Marie saw Papa as she came to the end of the stairs. He was bowing his head in prayer so Marie and Alice held hands and joined them in their prayer. Everyone scattered then and found their own places to sleep. Alice changed her clothing behind the canvas set up for their privacy but Marie insisted she would not change a clout as long as she was on this trip except for underclothes of course. She would change those sometime during the day. She would not be in her nightclothes if everyone had to abandon the ship in a storm or some other catastrophe. Marie and Alice found a space at the end of the ship's floor and slept well all night. They didn't even hear all the people who had to run up to the deck as they were seasick. Marie went to sleep still thanking God for rescuing them through the benevolence of Colonel Oglethorpe.

They woke up to the smell of coffee brewing. Marie looked over to Alice who was still sleeping. Her blond hair was clinging to the pillow. Marie thanked the Lord for another day and for the privilege of finding a friend on board this ship. She hoped Papa had found a place to sleep out of the wind. Marie folded her light blanket and put it on top of her pillow. She retrieved her brush and brushed her hair as she sat on the pillow. Alice finally heard her and looked over to her new friend. "Good Morning, Marie," she said as she stood up to go to the privacy place to change her clothes. There was someone behind the canvass right now but she needed to change before doing anything else. "Marie, I did sleep well but I heard a lot of people running up to the deck. I felt so sorry for them because I know they were sick all night. Did you hear anything?"

Marie flipped her hair out of her eyes as she continued to brush it. "I didn't hear anything, Alice. I guess I was so tired and I just put myself in God's hands while I went right to sleep."

Alice turned and ran toward the canvass as she saw another lady coming out. She quickly dressed and came back to her place beside Marie. "Let's go up on deck, Marie. We need some fresh air. I can hardly breathe. This is terrible. I hope someone will clean up down here."

Marie was laughing at her. "Just be glad we didn't get sick, Alice. I agree with you and we need to get some of that coffee so just wait until I get straightened out and put my hair up in a bun. I have another clip if you need it too."

"No, Marie…I just think I will push it back over my shoulders… maybe later on I could try it. I was never able to have anything for my hair. One of the jailors brought me a comb but I have even lost that. I usually just run my fingers through my hair and try to keep it out of my eyes." Alice noticed how Marie did her hair and thought she might borrow a hair clip to get her hair in order.

The girls weaved their way through the sleeping passengers as they made their way to the staircase. They found out it was a better day than yesterday. The ocean seemed calm and the ship seemed to move easily. Marie looked for Papa and finally saw him talking to Ted Miller.

"Good Morning, Papa. I hope you had a good night and also you, Mr. Miller. Alice and I were wondering how you could sleep with all these people getting sick and running up to the deck. I guess it will be better for you in the days ahead. Their stomachs just need to get used to the motion." Marie looked around to see all the beautiful ocean and blue sky. She was wondering where John Mason had slept for the night. She hoped to talk to him again and find out about his native country of Ireland. She could not find him all morning but spent the time getting more acquainted with Alice. She had not been jailed for as long as Marie but her time had been much lonelier. Alice thought she would die there too but that wasn't God's plan for her.

"I was wishing God would take me too, Marie," Alice said as they walked along the deck and found a place on the lee side of the ship where they could get out of the wind. "Then I would be encouraged when one of the jailors was kind enough to give me a comb or I would hear an Irish tenor singing about God's love."

Alice and Marie continued their conversation where they could hear an Irish tenor singing about God's love. "When I was jailed, Marie, I could hear that same voice as we hear now. Listen…I felt at that time he was talking to me and telling me how much Jesus loved me. My parents were always so busy going to parties and entertaining guests. I sometimes felt closer to the servants than I did my own parents."

Marie was so glad Alice had survived her jail time and to think she was all alone…but then we are never alone. God is right there with us. She hoped Alice would let her help with her hair. Marie knew when Alice would have meals she would regain her health and beauty. "Your experience is so much like mine, Alice. I was just as lonely but I always enjoyed going to London with my parents. They always bought me gifts and Mother was so much fun except the last time we were there. She seemed afraid to spend money and I couldn't understand it. I am afraid I wasn't very nice to her that time. I was so used to getting my own way. After I asked Jesus to come into my heart, I asked them to forgive me. It seemed every day I would wonder if they forgave me and if God could forgive me so I would tell them I was sorry again and again. Finally Papa said that once was enough. They had forgiven me and God had forgiven me. He said as far as the east is from the west so far has God removed my sin from me. I was so glad Mother kept reading to us from the Bible and explaining all these things to me. We were so afraid the jailor would take it away from us so every time we heard him coming we would hide it. I'm so glad you are a Christian also, Alice. If God saw us through all those years in jail he will be with us in this new land also. Did you hear some of the sailors talking about Indians? We will probably need God's protection in taking over this place."

Alice and Marie enjoyed their new friendship. Before long it was time to eat their mid-day meal. Marie still did not see John Mason. It was evening before Marie could talk to John. Marie and Alice enjoyed the day together but Alice was so tired she went down to retire for the night. The night sky was so beautiful and Marie wanted to stay out for awhile. John Mason found her looking over the ocean. He was feeling better this evening and he needed to get some sleep tonight but just wanted to get a bit of fresh air first. He paused to see Marie gazing out over the ocean. He realized how she had suffered all those 16 years in prison. He had only been there for five years. He was so thankful that all the passengers were going to have another chance for their lives. One of Marie's combs had slipped out of her hair and lay on the deck floor. Her beautiful black hair was coming out of the style she so painstakingly put it up that morning. John took this opportunity to walk up to her and pick up the comb.

"Excuse me, Miss but here is your comb that fell from your hair. I knew you didn't want to lose it."

"Oh, thank you. It was too beautiful out here to go inside. Alice was all worn out so she went in and Papa is sleeping soundly in his hammock out here somewhere," she said as she invited John to join her sightseeing. "Did you get enough sleep last night? Most of the passengers were running up and down the stairs. They were so sick. I am surprised that Alice and I did not get sick. It disturbed Alice though. That is why she retired early." As she turned to look at him she had to look up to his 6-foot height. She really liked his red hair. He looked as malnourished as everyone else but by the time they reached the Georgia colony she hoped they would all look better.

"I'm afraid I didn't fare out as well as you and Alice then. I was really sick all night. I found an out of the way corner to put my hammock near the bow of the ship. Marie…May I call you by your first name? I don't think your father would want you out here all alone."

"Yes, you can call me Marie. We shouldn't have to be formal here. I will call you by your first name too. I guess I never thought I could not be safe here alone but at the same time I really don't know all the passengers or the sailors. I suppose I better not take any more chances."

"I'm glad you have found a friend. I know you and your father were jailed a lot longer than Alice or me but we all missed out on our most important years. I was working on my first assignment in Ireland. I was so pleased to be sent to England to deliver a package to a business. It turned out to be illegal business and I was thrown in jail. It is so nice to be able to talk to someone again."

"I always enjoyed your singing and I could tell that you were a Christian also. I was so grieved when the one jailer stopped you from singing. Maybe I can bring Alice and you could sing some songs to us in the morning," Marie said as she prepared to go down to the hold.

"That will be great, Marie. I love to sing Irish songs but I especially like to sing songs of praise to our Lord. We could get more people and have a ship concert. There might be others who like to sing," John said as Marie walked toward the stairs.

They had their concert the next day and found other passengers who could sing. Rev. Shubert joined them and had morning devotions for them. Day after day would go the same way and everyone enjoyed the companionship. Colonel Oglethorpe was encouraged by their attitude toward each other because he knew they would have to work together to establish the city of Savannah, Georgia.

Each day brought them nearer to their destination. They constantly talked about the new land and how they would use their talents to make a living there. It was a new start and they never forgot to give thanks for the blessing of starting over. It went into December and it seemed proper and fitting to have celebration for Christmas. They knew it would not be the same as they had experienced at home before they were put into jail but it would be a time they could have a special service for Christmas and Rev. Shubert would be more than willing to make the service special for them.

John Mason had talked to Marie extensively and they looked for each other every morning. John knew early on that he had fallen in love with Marie. It wasn't the same as having the leisure to court her. They were both in their 30's and needed to get on with their lives. He planned to approach her father before he asked for her hand in marriage. He really liked her father and hoped that it would work out to join him in doing some kind of work to be self supporting. He had something for Marie's Christmas gift from him. He found the opportunity to talk to Marie's father on Christmas Eve day. John Martin was so glad Marie had found a Christian man. If it led to marriage it would be an answer to his prayers along with her mother.

"I have noticed your interest in my daughter, John. I have been impressed with the way you have participated in our devotionals every morning. Marie is bubbling over with all the nice things she says about you. It is so early to plan a lifetime commitment but she talked about you for years as you would sing her to sleep at night. I think you must be the man God has sent to be her husband. If she consents, Christmas would be a nice time to announce your intentions. You have my blessing," he said as he shook John's hand.

John found Marie standing alone on deck looking over the ocean. He stopped to admire her beauty. Her hair was shining in the moonlight. He had never expressed his feelings to her yet. He wondered if in due time she would want to start her new life with him. If this was true love, he would want her father to be with them also or on property near them,. Marie turned to see John gazing at her. She knew she should really go down to join Alice. She should not be here alone.

"John, I didn't know you were there. I was going in soon. I know we talked about being out here alone. It is so peaceful out here."

John walked to the lee side of the ship where Marie had found a quiet place to view the ocean. She pointed out the stars and how so long ago the shepherds were told by the angels that Christ was born. Tomorrow would be their Christmas dinner on board ship and their time with the other passengers.

"Marie, I would like to think God is bringing us together. Each day I see another reason to love you." John drew closer to Marie and as she turned to him, he drew her to him. Marie snuggled up to him and she thought she just fit. It seemed so right. She knew she loved him also. "I know this is too soon to declare my love but Marie, I almost feel I have known you for years. I could hear your family talk and cry. I would listen to the scripture read. It was hard sometimes to hear with all the commotion from other cells but what you discussed in scripture touched my heart and I heard your sweet mother explain scripture to you. One day I knelt in my cell and prayed for forgiveness, asking Jesus into my heart."

As Marie looked up at him with tears in her eyes, she hugged him again as she replied, "John, this is like a dream come true. I marvel at God's leading us together. The answer of course is yes. I truly love you, dear and it would be impossible for me to think of anyone who would bring me happiness more than you."

John kissed her as they looked forward to their future together. "You know, darling that I would always want to look after your father. If it wasn't for him and your mother, I wouldn't have you. I have already discussed this with your father and he gave me permission to ask you. Thank you for accepting me," and he kissed her again. Alice came up to look for Marie but quickly turned back when she saw John with her. Alice knew this was coming. She could see the love they had for each other.

John wanted to give Marie a special Christmas present. He looked through his meager possessions and found a necklace his mother had given him just before he was put into jail. He was successful in hiding it from the jailors and he knew he had found just the lady he wanted to have it. Everyone brought something to make their day special. The cooks made up a fruitcake from all their dried fruits.

The next morning was their Christmas dinner and Christmas meeting. Marie and John announced their engagement. John put the beautiful necklace around her neck. She looked up at him in surprise. "Don't ask me how I was able to keep this necklace that belonged to my mother. The stone is an emerald and it brings back so many memories of my home in Ireland. Please wear it as my promise to you." He bent down and kissed her and everyone clapped as they wished them happiness. "John, I don't have much for you but I knitted these socks for you, she said as she gave them to him. John was surprised and declared it was the one gift he really needed. " I made Papa a pair also. I hope he will like them." The message that day was great as it explained the sacrifice God had come down to them through Jesus' birth and they were celebrating His great love.

"I will always remember this as the greatest Christmas celebration that I ever had." John said as they left the Christmas meeting to have some time alone before retiring. "I hope someday I can show you Ireland but in the meantime let this emerald in the necklace remind you of my homeland."

John walked to the lee side of the ship where Marie had found a quiet place to view the ocean. "We did have a nice time today despite the lack of the right kind of foods and presents, Marie. I don't know how you managed to knit those socks for me. I have them on now and they are so warm and comfortable."

Marie laughed as she told him that Alice had given her the yarn. She had wondered when he left the meeting for a few minutes but now she understood he just wanted to try the socks. "A friend of the family had visited me just before we left and gave me yarn and a few other things. She said they were so sorry her parents had died before this opportunity came about. She wanted to share some of these presents with me."

"I told you before, I was able to save a few things also when I was picked up and put into jail I wanted you to have this necklace that belonged to my mother. The emerald stone brings back so many memories of my home in Ireland. I was picked up Marie, because they mistakenly thought I was with a gang of troublemakers. I think God is bringing us together and each day I love you more than ever." John drew closer to Marie and as she turned to him, he drew her to him and as Marie snuggled up to him, she thought as usual she just fit and it seemed so right. She knew she loved him also. John noticed the necklace around her neck as he bent to kiss her in the moonlight.

"John, this will be a Christmas that I will never forget if I live to be one hundred. It will always be in my heart and mind. Thank you so much for your love and for the necklace. I feel like I could stay with you forever." You could see the emerald shining in the moonlight. They felt the presence of God and His blessing on their lives.

John kissed her again. "You know, darling that I would always want to look after your father. I want you to be happy. We talked about this before and I enjoy talking to your father .I know I will enjoy working with him also". John hugged her closer as he said, "Oh, Marie, God has led us to this point in our lives and together we can put all our suffering behind us. I know we will have a good life together and look to our Lord for His leading and direction. Thank you for accepting me. I will buy you a ring as soon as we land and I make some money if there is a place to do that."

Marie laughed and quietly said, "The necklace tells me of your love, dear. I hate to leave you now but Alice will be wondering where I went if she wakes up. I will see you in the morning."

They both retired to their separate places and couldn't wait until morning to see each other again. Papa approved of their plans to get married and thanked God that they had met in this way. They had announced their engagement to everyone aboard ship and enjoyed the blessings of everyone there. They were soon in the New Year and coming closer to Georgia.

On January 15, 1733 they could see land. Colonel Oglethorpe explained to them that it was not their destination yet. It would be a temporary camp on Trenches Island off the South Carolina coast. They would be taking small boats up the Savannah River to reach the Yamacraw Bluff where they would settle. There was some discontentment but they trusted Colonel Oglethorpe to see that they settled in Georgia. In the meantime, they were greeted by some citizens of South Carolina. They were thrilled to welcome them to be their neighbors. This colony of Georgia would be a buffer between them and Florida. The assembly of South Carolina voted them a large supply of cattle and other provisions. The passengers of the Ship Anne put up tents for their temporary dwelling until Colonel Oglethorpe could see that everything was ready for them in the new colony. On February 1, 1733 the rangers sent boats…a sloop and five smaller boats. They proceeded down the inland waterway to the mouth of the Savannah River. They landed on the river bank of Savannah. A small force of rangers had constructed a stairway up the forty-foot high sandy embankment. Everyone was shouting and dancing with joy as they approached their destination. There were Indians lined up along the shore waiting for them. Colonel Oglethorpe told them that the Indians here were friendly and just wanted to welcome them.

John and Marie were seated together holding hands with Papa right there beside them. Alice was in the same boat with them as they came to the shore of the Georgia Colony. Only God knew what their destiny would be. Marie breathed a prayer of thanksgiving and a determination that she and John would always love God and each other.

Chapter 3

Marie looked up to the stairway and found it terribly discouraging to try climbing all those 40 feet of stairs. She was so afraid of heights and to think after coming all this distance to feel like turning back. It was better on Trench's Island where they had stayed until they were ready to have them come to the mainland. Everyone enjoyed camping out on the Island. The people from South Carolina even came there to welcome them to the New Land and to inform the Colonel of their help. The people of South Carolina were so good to them. They gave them cattle, chickens, seed for planting when the weather was warmer. Their guests of South Carolina told them they had brought the animals to the colony so they would be there when they arrived at their destination. Marie was concerned about her father. Would he be able to climb that many steps? She bowed her head and said a word of prayer for Papa.

"Marie, are you coming?" John asked. John had been the first person out of the boat. He was so anxious to be able to start putting this city of Savannah together. Colonel Oglethorpe had all the plans. John approached the boat again to help Marie out. Marie insisted Papa would get out first. John Mason did not start climbing the steps right away but waited for the others to get out of the boat. Marie's hands were trembling as John helped her out first after her father and then helped Alice. "Don't worry, Marie, we will all look after your father. Let's start up the stairs. If the rangers could build the stairs, I guess we can climb them".

They could see that Marie's father could not go all the way up the stairs without a rest. He was all out of breath so Marie stopped with him to give him a chance to catch his breath before continuing. John stopped too and also Alice. She wanted to see the new colony at the same time as Marie. Everyone else went by them. John leaned his head on the railing and soon had his breath again. "I'm so sorry keeping you two back like this but thank you anyway," he said as he started up the stairs again. They could see all the trees and the good land on each side of the steps as they climbed to the top.

The Indians greeted them as they came to the end, even giving them a hand to get up to the campsite. The Colonel was already opening up the tents and distributing them among the colonists. They would sleep much the same way they did on the Island. Colonel Oglethorpe had his own tent where he could conduct meetings with the men of the colony to appoint them their town lot in the square and also the fifty acre farm plot outside of the town. He also would be having meetings with the Indians. The colonists would be trading with John and Mary Musgrove from their trading house at the north end of the bluff. Everyone was busy getting settled. Alice and Marie were getting settled in one of the women's tents. They were finally feeling at home even though their town-lot was just getting selected and it would take time to have their own home. Papa went with John and the other men to put up their tent after seeing to the tent for the ladies. The Indians were walking around and trying to help them. They knew Colonel Oglethorpe from his former trips and they had built up good friendship with him. The Indians were dressed in their finest feathers and deerskin shirts and pants. Mr. Musgrove was the interpreter and even the King, Queen and Chiefs came to welcome the colonists to their new home. One of the Indian girls was intrigued with the ladies of the colonist group. Marie and Alice approached her to see if she knew any English.

"Thank you for coming to see us," Marie said and smiled at her. Alice kept looking around at the other Indians and when they didn't seem to care if one of their girls came to talk to them she joined Marie in conversing with the Indian maiden.

"I wish to thank you also. My name is Alice. What is your name? We would like to be friends."

Mary Musgrove saw the girls trying to get acquainted and walked over to them. "I know you can say some English, Star. Try to talk to them and I will help you." Star was very shy and yet she wanted to make friends with these girls. Her mother had told her all about who would be coming after talking to Colonel Oglethorpe when he was there to make the arrangements. Their chief, Tomochichi, made the treaty with the Colonel to settle the land although the chief insisted that he did not have the power to sell the land or to give it to them. He assured them of their friendliness but they could not speak for the other Indian tribes. He believed the land belonged to the God of all nature and they were free to live there with them. In half English and half Creek, Star welcomed the girls to their land. Her voice sounded like music to Marie and Alice. They understood her welcome and put their hands out to greet her. She looked as if she were in her early 20's. They asked her to come with them to their tent.

"My father, Cornstalk, will help you with planting and with the seed." Alice and Marie were surprised that she could communicate with them so well but they knew Mary Musgrove must have taught her to speak English.

"We are surprised you can speak English so well. We will try to learn your language as well." Marie said,"You know your hair and mine are about the same color," she said as she touched her own hair and indicated to Star they were alike.

Star smiled at that and turned to Alice with her blond hair. She had never seen anyone with that color hair. Star went over to touch her hair. It was so soft and wavy. The girls knew they would be friends.

Colonel Oglethorpe was finished his meeting with the Indians and came out of his tent to gather everyone together. He gave the Chief some gifts and the Indians wanted to entertain the new colonists so one of the Indians who was dressed with all kinds of feathers and rattles in his hands, was dancing all over the camping site, singing and throwing his body into a thousand different postures. Everyone was glad he had come to make them feel at home but by this time everyone was tired and ready to go to their tents for the night.

Colonel Oglethorpe bid the new colonists Good Night and told them work would start at sunup tomorrow for everyone. Even the ladies would be able to do something to start making Savannah their new home.

The night was very short for Alice and Marie. They had been exhausted when they went to bed and didn't wake up until they heard the other ladies starting breakfast. "Marie, Marie, we are supposed to be helping. Hurry up," Alice said as she shook Marie awake.

"O dear, I am so sorry, Alice. I feel like my head just hit the pillow. I will hurry. Wait, you look like you are already dressed. Go ahead outside. I will be with you in a few minutes." Marie rushed and was out in no time. This was so great…like being a part of a big family. She just hoped everyone would cooperate and they would get a lot done today. She noticed they already had built two necessaries out under the trees and away from the camp side.

Colonel Oglethorpe was standing with a cup of coffee while the ladies were preparing side meat and fresh eggs for breakfast. Everyone had their pewter and trenchers handy to be ready to eat when it was finished. As all the people gathered around the cooking fire, the Colonel asked Rev. Shubert to ask the blessing on the food.

Rev. Shubert would be going back on the next ship heading for England. Marie was praying another minister would come to take his place. In the meantime Rev. Shubert served as their Pastor and he wanted to help build the city. Everyone bowed their heads as he thanked God again for the safe trip here and asked God's blessing on the food and thanks for all the help from the people of South Carolina and the Indian tribe.

Ruth Miller was filling their pewter dishes with fresh eggs, (thanks to the people of South Carolina who gave them chickens and side meat along with some hard biscuits.) Soon everyone was finished eating and ready to proceed with tasks at hand.

Ted Miller was reading off all the work assignments that Colonel Oglethorpe had written down to be accomplished. "He tells me, citizens of Savannah, we need to finish our tents and get some of our stores on shore. This will probably take us all day and remember we will stop our duties tomorrow on Sunday and attend divine service in Mr. Oglethorpe's tent. He would like to be considered one of us and would prefer that we forget the title of Colonel for now and just call him Mr. Oglethorpe. He will be working alongside us and hopes to be able to see this community completed soon. The people from South Carolina will be coming to help us. They have given us livestock and some food. They also plan to send some of their slaves along to help. We all know that it is against our law to own any slaves but we are accepting their help right now. The Indians have volunteered to help also. We need to always keep our friendship with the Creek Indians living near here. The plans are all laid out and there will be a job for everyone."

"Thank you, Ted." Mr. Oglethorpe advanced to the front of the group. "We need some men to fell the necessary trees for building our houses. Our community will be laid out in squares with a town lot and 500 acres outside of the town for farming. There will be a square in the center and places for business. We will need blacksmiths, brick makers, cabinetmakers, carpenters, shoemakers, printers, basket makers, gunsmiths and many other specialists in addition to the farmers. The first thing to be taken care of next week are the palisades around the place of our settlement as a fence in case we should be attacked by the Indians or Spanish in Florida, while others of us will be employed in clearing the lines and cutting trees to the proper length for the palisades. Our fortress will protect us from all harm." Everyone went to do the Colonel's bidding after finishing breakfast. The ladies were taking care of cleaning up and planning the next meals besides getting all the tents in order. Ruth Miller seemed to be in charge of the ladies work. She asked them to bring water for the workers. Everyone wanted to cooperate as Ruth had such a sweet way of asking for their help.

As Marie and Alice were taking water from the spring near by, Star came to talk to them. She gladly took her part in bringing the water. They rounded up the cows and goats to bring them to the water also.

Their day went well and Star stayed right with Marie and Alice. Star helped with the cooking and went home right after the supper meal. She said if they wanted to learn how to make baskets she would bring her mother along and she could show them what to use for the reed.

Marie had not seen John all day but they knew it would be like this. The men did not come in yet for their evening meal. She hoped to see John and Papa before she retired for the night. Alice was so tired that Marie bid her good night and sat down with the ladies that were still finishing their supper and feeding the children. Marie helped with some of the children and walked with them to their tents so they could go to bed. She looked up when she came out of one of the tents to see the men all hurrying back to the campsite. She went to get Papa a trencher of food and John went over to get his own. She could tell John was tired also but he smiled at her and winked. She could just see the love in his eyes. She was so grateful to God for leading her to the right person to marry. It was getting dark but after Marie saw that Papa was taken care of she and John went over to the tree they had marked with their names. They sat on the ground while John ate his meal. The hearts were still on the tree with their initials. "I guess you are tired too, Marie. You all made it easier for us to stay out in the woods to cut the wood in the lengths Mr. Oglethorpe wanted. We know he has spent a lot of time planning this city. He knew we needed to be fortified first so we will be ready to start that on Monday. I guess it is sunup to sundown for our workdays. You look tired, honey. I know the women were all doing so much also." He looked around the area as more and more people were retiring for the night. He knew this was a day that would go down in history. All taking part would never forget it…all the blessings of working together and all the sorrows of losing some as they crossed the ocean and finally came to the site where Colonel Oglethorpe had spent so much time arranging their settlement in this land. His prayer was, "May God truly bless this colony."

"God has really been with us on this trip, providing for our every need. I know you are tired too, Marie, but just think how nice it would be to have our own home and the freedom is just unbelievable. We will have the very first wedding here. We will have a clapboard house. We have some of the trees already felled and ready to go. Of course the fortifications come first so we will be safe from the other Indian tribes and even the Spanish would like to take over this land. That is why the people from South Carolina have helped us so much. They are looking for a better way to keep their colony safe from the Spanish in Florida. We would be a buffer for them. As they know we are here they would be discouraged to bother the people in South Carolina in any way. Honey, I think I will sign up for the carpenter job. I can learn a lot from the older men and continue even after the settlement is completed." Marie listened as her fiancée planned their future with her.

"I will help as I am needed for now, John. I would really like to learn how to spin yarn and weave it into material. That will be after we are married and settled in our new home. It seems like a dream that I met you, John." They were both so tired that they decided it was time to go to their tents. John held her close as they stood up to bid each other a goodnight.

"Goodnight, Sweetheart. I love you so much and even now I think I love you more each day." Their kisses were long until Marie forced herself to walk to her tent. Alice was still awake and waiting for Marie. She thought this relationship was so exciting and she just thanked God for sending her two good friends.

The girls settled down in their beds as Marie said, "This is so exciting, Alice. We will be married as soon as our house is ready. Of course most of the men will be working on the forts now but John is hearing so much about carpentry that he wants to go into it after we are finished here. I can see you are so tired, Alice so I will bid you goodnight." Alice was almost asleep but she was glad for her friend's happiness. She knew God would have someone for her in the right time. She turned over and went to sleep knowing that in the morning would be the first service in their new homeland.

Everyone was packed into Colonel Oglethorpe's tent the next day for services. There was so much unity and thanksgiving among the people gathered in their leader's tent. Rev. Shubert was there to give the message.

Colonel Oglethorpe said, "We are so privileged to have a Pastor right with us through the whole trip getting here. As I walked around viewing the work we did on the first day here, I was so impressed. You looked like you were all working together to get ready building the forts this week. If we persevere you will have the city you always dreamed of. God has been good to us. I noticed your language was good as I walked around. I didn't know you all had so many skills. Thank you all for coming and I will turn it over to Rev. Shubert."

"I will ask John Martin to open in prayer. Here is a man who suffered so many years in prison and then lost his wife there. His faith stood firm and he would say that he and his daughter give all the credit to God as his wife who took one day at a time and was in constant communion with the Lord. She will meet him in Heaven."

John Martin arose and Marie smiled at him to give encouragement to him. He had never professed to be a preacher but had learned that God was with him through all his problems and he was so grateful. "Here we are, dear Lord, standing in our promised land and just as you guided the children of Israel through the wilderness, you have guided us here. We pray that your will might be done in everything we do here. Thank you for Colonel Oglethorpe's help and also King George the second for listening and releasing us from prison. May you bless our colony and all the colonies here with freedom and help us to stay well as we work together to found this colony of Georgia. May the words of our mouth and the meditation of our hearts be acceptable in thy sight, O Lord, our strength and our redeemer. Amen."

You could hear a pin drop as John sat down beside Marie and his future son in-law, John Mason. Rev. Shubert stood in the center of the group and gave his sermon on God's mercy and love to his people.

The Sunday continued with fellowship and eating in one of the larger tents. It was cold on this February day so they moved back all the bedrolls and discussed what the days work would be tomorrow. John and Marie finished their meal and took a walk even in the colder weather. They knew there would not be a lot of time to be together this week. While Alice was greeting their new Indian friend, Star, they walked the other way and discussed their future together. They could hardly wait until their home was built. Hand in hand they explored some more of their settlement and chose the place they wanted their home to be built. Star and Alice talked as much as they could with their language barrier. Star was learning more English words all the time.

The next day their firearms were delivered to them from the store. Each man was given a musket, bayonet, cartridge box and belt. All those able to bear arms lined up to receive their arms. They were given the times and places where they should be to guard the settlement. Each family was given a bible, three wooden bowls, a frying pan and a common prayer book.

It was March 1st. when the first house in the square was framed and raised, with Mr. Oglethorpe driving the first pin. The trees had been cut down and crosscut into proper lengths for clapboards and then splitting them in order to build clapboard houses. One by one the houses were finished and taken over by their owners. John Martin had the house next to Marie and John's home. They had built a chapel also and finally in May after the planting was completed, Marie and John decided to get married.

It was a beautiful day on this Saturday of 1733. John Martin was so glad his daughter would be married to a Christian man. He had come to know him so much more since they had landed in Georgia. It was a pleasure to work with him and to find him so considerate of everyone as they worked with the other men, some who were accomplished carpenters but some who were learning the trade as they worked. God had provided the couple with a house and farmland. As they would be living right next door to Marie's father, they would be able to look after him. John Martin was ready to take his daughter down the aisle as the first bride to be married in this new chapel. He stood at the door watching for his daughter. She was standing with Alice and Star in front of the Chapel on the cobblestone road they had constructed throughout the town.

"Oh, Star I just love this dress your mother has made for me." Her dress was made of deerskin. Star was explaining how her mother had made the dress and also the dresses for Alice and Star. All three of the girls also had matching moccasins. The dress was decorated with all kinds of beadwork and fringe, also the white moccasins that went with the dress. Alice helped Marie with her hair and it looked beautiful peeking through her lacey cap. They were all glad that Rev. Shubert did not leave yet so he performed the ceremony. He felt like he knew everyone there as he had watched them work and ministered to them as they constructed this town of Savannah. He had noticed the friendliness between these girls and this beautiful Indian girl.

Marie and John had decided to have an Indian wedding. They needed two couples to act as sponsors for the marriage. The couples would promise to watch over them and to be there for them if they needed any advice. The couple would be promising that they would never seek a divorce but always ask God to lead them and to seek help from the two couples. Ted and Ruth Turner would be one of the couples' chosen and Cornstalk and Spring would be the other couple chosen. Star was glad her parents had consented to do this. They walked into the chapel to sit in the front and wait for the bride and her father to walk up the aisle. The groom along with the Pastor was already at the front waiting for the bride to come down the aisle.

Marie motioned for the girls to go before her and start up the stairs to the church door. Marie was happy to see Papa waiting for her at the door but she was also sad that Mother could not be with her on this very important day in her life. Mother had enjoyed John's singing also as they were in the confines of the prison. Dabbing at the tears in her eyes with this special wedding handkerchief, she determined to face the future with the love and faith that her mother had faced life with.

John Martin stood ready to assist his daughter up the steps and the girls went before her as the music played and Marie followed the girls up the aisle accompanied by her father. John Martin remembered times before they went to prison when he and Elizabeth despaired at the greed and selfish times Marie showed in her growing up years. She had worked along with the other women here in Savannah and had shown the love of Jesus in her heart. John praised God for his beautiful daughter. Her black hair peaking through the lace cap glittered in the sunlight. Her slim form showed to advantage the Indian dress. The wild flowers that she carried told of the nature of this colony they were settling. Papa escorted Marie down the aisle. He whispered to her, "Marie, if you have any doubts about your marriage now is the time you can back out. You need to be sure." Marie just shook her head no, and smiled at him. She wanted to be with John for the rest of her life.

It was a beautiful wedding and Marie would always treasure the wedding book that she received from the Pastor. He closed the service with a poem:

Equality

They were so one, it never could be said
Which one of them ruled, or which of them obeyed
He ruled because she would obey and she,
By him obeying, ruled as well as he.
There ner'er was known between them a dispute
Save which the other's will should execute.
No jealousy their down of love o'ercast,
Nor blasted were their wedded days with strife;
Each season looked delightful, as it passed,
To the fond husband and the faithful wife.—Beattie

Rev. Shubert pronounced them man and wife as he gave the marriage book to the bride. In the book were poems and advice on their marriage along with their marriage certificate.

The sun was going down as they went outdoors and Marie noticed a beautiful bluebird in the tree nearby. Star told her it was a bluebird of happiness and it foretold the happiness they would share as a married couple. John was impressed with the Indian way of looking at life. They seemed to see a reason for all nature. They would not put their trust in the medicine man but put their trust in Jesus as their Saviour. Everyone there was congratulating them on their marriage and going to the home of John Martin where the ladies of the town had prepared a wedding supper for them and their guests. As the crowd walked to his home, John felt the presence of his wife and mother of his daughter. She would have rejoiced in this marriage. The wedding cake made by Ruth Miller was beautiful. Marie couldn't get over how much work the ladies went to just for her and her husband, John. They had also been working on a quilt that they did not want her to see so she surmised the quilt was a wedding present. She could hardly wait to see the quilt. She prayed that God would bless them all. This May 25, 1733 as written in her marriage book would always be the highlight of her life.

Chapter 4

It was a winter day on this December 24 of 1738 as Marie looked out of the window while she was giving Rebecca a bath. Time had passed quickly and each day was worked from sun-up to sun-down. God had blessed their marriage these past five years with so much joy, giving them two children, George and Rebecca. George was playing quietly on the floor with his blocks. He didn't know what to make of Rebecca. "Mama" he asked, "When will Rebecca play with me?" George was three years old now and could put sentences together, astonishing his Mom and Dad. Marie talked while she bathed her baby girl, thinking how she would have loved a baby sister or brother. "She is only three months old, George. You will have to wait until she is bigger to have a playmate."

As she finished bathing her, glancing out of the window, she could see John up on the roof of the house they were building down the street. Everything had gone the way Colonel Oglethorpe planned for this city of Savannah. John enjoyed carpentry and always took good care of his tools. He had his own saw, broadax, awl, mallet, plane, drawknife, gimlet and frow. He had so many different woods to choose from. They had plenty of oak, locust, tulip, yellow pine, cypress, juniper, and chestnut. Marie especially liked the oak for the doors and the furniture John had made for her. She liked making baskets from this beautiful wood also. Star still came over to make baskets with her even though she had her own family now. Bright Arrow had come to work with John and met Star. From all appearances, it was love at first sight. Star still helped in the store and Bright Arrow was learning carpentry from John. He was using John's tools until he made enough money for his own which should be soon. The clapboard was cut and waiting for the men to use.

Star and Bright Arrow had their first baby in the spring. Marie received news of the birth as she was watching the first bluebird making a nest in their oak tree. She knew she would see the blue eggs soon and then the nestlings. She would point out the mother bird to George and they would rush out each day to see the next thing happening to the bird. The daddy bird had nothing to do with the making of the nest or nestling the eggs. George had been glad when the little birds hatched but sad when they were big enough to leave the nest.

It was a cool day on this Christmas Eve day as she was recalling all these things that had happened over the years. This would be Rebecca's first Christmas. She remembered the Christmas of 1736 when John Wesley came to be their Pastor. Several of her friends came to know the Lord through his ministry. There was so much love felt throughout Savannah the Christmas John Wesley came. He wanted to minister to the Indian tribe too and she was glad Star heard him at their tribal meeting and said she knew now how her Christian friends had the peace and joy that she didn't have at times. She decided then to be a Christian and even though she was a new Christian she was a beautiful testimony in her Indian tribe.

Marie wrapped Rebecca up in a towel and looked out of the window again at her husband on the roof. "Oh, look at your Daddy now, George. He had his hat on when he left but now his red hair is shining in the sunlight and his hat is on the ground. He just needs someone to follow him all around so that he takes care of himself. He needs to come in early too because we are going to have so much fun, George. You have been a good boy, honey so you should get something for Christmas." George put one more block on his tower and clapped his hands in glee.

Marie dressed baby Rebecca, nursing her first and then put her in the cradle for her morning nap. She stopped to play with George and show other ways to build with the blocks. She showed him how to pretend he was building a house just as his daddy was doing. She still wanted to make some pies. They had enough dried apples to do just that. As she considered the foods to get ready for Christmas she noticed John climbing down the ladder he had made for the job. He seemed to be heading for home so she rushed out to open the door for him. George immediately ran over to John. "Daddy, Daddy! You're home. I building too…just like you." John stooped down to pick up his little son.

"Oh, Marie…it is so cold out there. I'm trying to decide if we will call it quits at noon or what. Bright Arrow was hammering some of the clapboard and has injured his hand. He was trying to get the overlap of ½ inch on the clapboard and hit his hand nailing the roof. I need something to wrap his hand in…there, that's fine," he said as Marie handed him a clean cloth.

"Your hands are so cold, honey. Why don't you just stop now? We're having a Christmas Eve supper tonight. Bright Arrow and Star are coming too. You said that you were ahead of schedule anyway." Marie knew John would get so interested in his building that he forgot to take care of his health.

"It sounds like a good idea, Marie, and I don't think Bright Arrow will complain. He is ready to go back home to Star and their baby. I'll be here for lunch," and he set George down giving him a hug as he hurried back with the cloth to bind up Bright Arrow's hand.

George looked so sad but went back to his blocks. He liked to have his daddy play with him. John was always telling how maybe one day he would join him making houses in this town of Savannah. John had told him this since the time he was born and he didn't know how much George understood yet. Marie knew John had a lot of plans for his son.

Marie went back to her plans for Christmas Eve meal. This would be the first Christmas without her dad. He had died last year from pneumonia. They thought it was his working in the cold weather and not taking care of himself. They all missed him and George especially missed his grandpa coming in to see him. Grandpa

John had been so thankful for his grandson and would tell him all about his grandma that never lived to see her grandson. How she would have loved him!

Marie went about getting her baking pans out and starting the two pies she wanted for their dessert. Alice was coming also. There seemed to be a young English fellow in Alice's life. He was coming with Alice for the Christmas Eve meal. She didn't know how serious the two were but he was coming to church with Alice and seemed a good match for her.

Marie could smell the bread baking. She was so thankful for the oven John had made for her as part of the fireplace. She was cooking the dried apples when John came in from working on the house they were building.

"Mmm...smells really good in here, honey," John said as he opened the oaken door. "Guess we will call it quits. Thought I might help you get ready for our guests." Marie looked up from mixing the dough for the pies.

"I'm just glad you are in from that cold weather, John. I guess Bright Arrow was glad to get home with his bandaged hand. Do you think it is serious? I hope they will be able to come tonight. As soon as you wash up and change I will have the lunch ready. We will be eating late tonight," she said as she lay the pie dough in the pan and running over to the oven to take the bread out. "I guess I could use your help, honey. George has been so good but I still am behind on all the things I want to do before our guests come tonight. George didn't slow me up at all. I couldn't use that as an excuse."

John went laughing into the bedroom to change. He was thankful they could have more than one room. He had really worked hard to build it just the way they wanted it. Colonel Oglethorpe even was impressed with his work. John looked down at his little daughter in the cradle. How small she was---the very image of Marie. Marie had told him of her childhood and how spoiled she was. Also, how she longed for brothers and sisters but her mother had said that it wasn't in God's plans.

John dressed quickly and joined Marie and George. He went over to Marie working so hard to make this Christmas special. Her face was flushed with the heat she felt as she put the pies in the oven. Her bread was already out to cool.

"My, this fire in the fireplace feels good. Everything smells delicious, Marie," John said as he kneeled down beside George. George was thrilled his dad was home. "Now let's put the blocks away, George and have lunch…then we can string the popcorn Mama made for the Christmas tree. George liked to help his daddy put the toys away. Everything had a place in their small home. John always said, "A place for everything and everything in its place makes for a safe house and a happy family.' Before long George was getting into the chair his daddy had made just for him and waiting for his lunch. Marie was getting the chicken soup dipped from the kettle hanging in the fireplace.

"I still am so thankful for the people in South Carolina providing the cattle and the chickens they gave us to start. They have multiplied to make us enough to eat and we have never gone without food." Marie turned to John with the ladle in her hand as she tested the soup to see if it was ready. It felt boiling to her hand. "Guess it is ready. Would you get our trenchers out for the soup, John? I'll put the kettle on the table. The pies are in the oven so we can eat now".

John loved his wife dearly. He put a lot of love into the home he built for them and also all the furniture. The beautiful hutch he built was the envy of the whole community. Marie sat down on the bench with John and they all joined hands to ask God to bless this food. Marie cut a piece of bread for each one to eat with their soup. "We will save all the best food for tonight, Christmas Eve, and George, we will hear about the baby Jesus tonight. Daddy will read it right out of the Bible." George looked up from eating, smiling at his parents. It wasn't long until George was rubbing his eyes and yawning. "I'll lay him down for his nap, Marie. He is so tired. He will be ecstatic tonight." And John carried him in to their bed for his much needed nap.

They would have a good time but Marie needed help. John went over to Marie as she was clearing the table and keeping watch over her pies. "What can I do now to help you, darling?" he asked as he turned Marie around and hugged her. "Oh, it is so good to have you at home, John," she said as she returned his hugs. "I want to pop some more corn so we can decorate our tree. We will wait until George is up from his nap to start decorating the tree. Maybe you can pop the corn. I was getting the food prepared for tonight. I know Rebecca will be up from her nap any minute now. Let's see…. The corn is in the bin over there. Pop only enough for the tree right now. We will pop more tonight for eating after our Christmas Eve dinner."

"I will get right to it, Marie. You know anymore you have so much work to do around here. I guess it would be nice to have some help. Andy Robinson bought a slave to help his wife in the kitchen. It is working for them. Of course, they have a lot more children than we do."

Marie was startled that John would even think it was good to own a slave after their experiences in England. "Oh, John, I don't think you know what you are saying. We are against slavery and we agreed with Colonel Oglethorpe that it was wrong when the people from South Carolina sent their slaves in to help us. Remember, when we first came here. It runs shivers down my back when I think of anyone wanting to own another person. Just remember why we are here. It is terrible when your freedom is taken away from you. My heart just grieves for them. I know slave owners would say that they take care of their slaves and treat them well but that doesn't take away the loss they must feel. No, John, we will never own slaves. Mr. Robinson must have a lot more money than we have anyway if he can afford a slave."

John didn't realize how terrible Marie thought slavery was and how it reminded her of her own time in Debtors Jail. "I'm sorry, Marie. I didn't mean to say anything to hurt you or to bring you back to that terrible time we had and you were in there so much longer than I. We will never own slaves but there is nothing we can do to prevent others from bringing them in. A lot of the new residents came from South Carolina and brought their slaves with them. Colonel Oglethorpe never wanted slaves to be here either but when the people from South Carolina came in here to help they brought their slaves along and I don't think we could have cleared as much ground without them," and John put another hopper of popped corn into the basket Marie had given him for that purpose.

Marie took another pie out of the oven and set it down on the table. "I know you wouldn't own anyone, John. I guess I get all worked up when I see them here. Colonel Oglethorpe didn't want any alcohol sold here either but I know some in our city have purchased some at Mary's store and brought it here because Star was telling me about it. Star would never drink and I don't think Bright Arrow would either. Both of them profess to be Christians and I know it is terrible when an Indian gets into the habit.

Wait a minute. I hear Rebecca. Well, I have to go change her and feed her before George wakes up." She paused to look into the basket John was putting the corn in. "I think that will be enough, dear. With the string of popcorn around the tree and the candles, it will be a Christmas Eve we will long remember."

Marie looked up at her six-foot tall husband and with all of her five feet five inches in height she looked into his eyes, "I am so happy here, John. How I love you and the children. God has blessed us greatly here." John set the basket down and drew her into his arms. "I am so glad Marie, but I think…You will have to go…Your daughter is getting impatient." He smiled as Marie rushed into the bedroom to take care of Rebecca.

A couple hours later they were all ready for the dinner and the evening with their friends. They were all dressed up for Christmas Eve. George had his Sunday knickers on with a shirt just like Daddy's. Marie had made them and spent many hours sewing special outfits for the whole family. George was so proud that he looked just like his daddy. He was sitting on a chair very proper and ready for the company. Marie brought the cradle in the front room where they lived except for sleeping. The table was all set with the pewter ware and the spoons. Star and Bright Arrow was the first couple to come. They brought baby Cornstalk with them. He was named after his grandfather. "Everything looks beautiful, Marie," Star said as she hugged her friend. What a nice tree! Do we all get to decorate it tonight?"

"Yes, we will all decorate it. John has the popcorn all popped and ready to string so maybe you can start stringing it, Star, and then the others can join in when they come. George can hardly wait until we start decorating the tree. We will eat before we decorate the tree and put the candles on it. You know how careful we have to be when the candles are burning."

It wasn't long until all the guests arrived. Everyone was seated at the table when John opened his Bible and read the Christmas story from Luke 2:1-20. Everyone was silent as the story of baby Jesus was read. Even George listened as his Daddy read the story. John closed then with a blessing for the food and thankfulness with the Lord's provision. Marie had prepared a delicious meal and Star had brought a large bowl of her Indian pudding. Ruth brought a Christmas cake. Ruth and Ted still did not have any children. No one knew and it was too soon to announce they were finally expecting a baby come Spring. They enjoyed seeing the other children. They would never forget the tragedy of losing their first baby in Debtor's Prison. It was so good to be with their friends. Everyone was having a good time. Marie roasted the chicken to perfection. The hard-boiled eggs were a special treat. Not everyone had chickens.

After the dinner everyone was ready to decorate the tree. Even George helped put the string of popcorn on the tree. In fact, he tried to eat some of the corn before Marie could take it from him. They sang Christmas carols and John's voice came through loud and clear with strains of the land of Ireland from which he came. To hear him sing brought so many memories to Marie of their days in the prison. She wanted to forget all of those thoughts but they were a part of her past and in a way made her a better Christian. She didn't think she could have endured the whole thing if she had not put her life in God's hands and through the Holy Spirit endured until they were released through the good planning of Colonel Oglethorpe. The tree was decorated now and all the candles were lit. It was beautiful.

Marie had a present for everyone. It was just a small remembrance. She had embroidered handkerchiefs on the linen material she had found in the store. The linen handkerchiefs were embroidered nicely with their initials in the corner. Alice had introduced her friend,

Charles Peck to everyone attending. Charles fit right in the group and had a good time. Charles had come over from England on the last trip Colonel Oglethorpe had made bringing some of the Indian tribe with him to meet the King. The Indians were impressed and the King was pleased that the Indians had so much respect for their country and for Colonel Oglethorpe although they were all glad to get back home to their Indian tribe.

All the ladies started clearing the pewter ware away from the table and helped Marie straighten things before departing for their homes. Soon everyone had gathered their outdoors clothes together and wrapped their babies up to go home. Alice and Charles stayed behind.

"We wanted to tell you, Marie, that Charles and I will be married soon." Marie and John gave them their blessing. They seemed made for each other and with their Christian testimony, they knew they would establish a good home in this new city. "I thought it was leading to something like this," John said.

"I guess you will be wanting us to build you a house soon." Alice looked to Charles to break the news to their good friends.

"I know Alice dreads telling you about our move but we will get married here and then we plan to live in Frederica. They are looking for new settlers there and they need more carpenters to build the city up. They already have their fort built but they are way behind with the housing. In fact some of them are enduring the winter in tents. We need the fort for even the protection of Savannah." Marie was startled at this announcement and went over to Alice.

"How I will miss you, Alice. I can see that your eyes are just sparkling with love for Charles but I thought you would live here." Marie's eyes were misty with tears as she looked at her dear friend and yet she wouldn't stand in her way to happiness. Charles was a very tall man and looked husky enough to be able to take on any job he was called upon to do. None of the men even here knew what time they would be called upon to defend their city. Charles was handsome with his blonde hair and sturdy build. He would make a good husband for Alice, Marie's dear friend. Marie looked to John to express their feelings.

"We are happy for you, Charles and we know you will have a Christian home. We give you our blessing and anything we can do we will try to help you. One thing I know, friend, you are a good carpenter and we remember your work with our crew. Let's join hands and pray for you right now." John took Marie's hand and Marie joined hands with Charles. As they bowed their heads in prayer, they felt close to God and knew they were following his purpose for their lives. With "Merry Christmas" as they parted, Marie and John saw them to the door. This was certainly a good Christmas, one they would never forget. As Marie lifted their little son, George off the floor where he had been playing with his blocks, she carried him to his bed. He had just lain down beside them and was sleeping. Rebecca was already in her crib. It was almost midnight by the time Marie and John had everything put away and presents under the tree. Hand in hand they went to their bedroom and retired for the night. Tomorrow would be an exciting day this December 25 of 1738.

Chapter 5

Star was the first one getting ready to go home on this April day of 1755. Star was so sorry about the news she heard of other Indian tribes joining with the French from Canada to hurt their white friends. Although it had not been officially declared, the French and Indian War was on. Everyone was on their guard especially in regard to the Indians as they were helping the French to claim parts of their land as New France. Star was so afraid her English friends would be hurt. So far some of her tribe had even threatened her friends. As usual, all the ladies enjoyed their time together and they were able to put the blocks together to be ready for quilting. Of course there was talk of this war between England and France. Although it had not been declared yet it was a sure thing that it would come about. The ladies usually let all this kind of discussion up to their husbands but it seemed closer to home all the time. The Indians were taking sides in the conflict also. Most of them were helping the French but some were really faithful to their American friends. Major Washington even went to the Ohio Country to ask the French to leave and of course they declined. They already had all the forts completed and were paying the Indians for the scalps they turned in. "I feel so sorry for the ladies and children that are close to the fighting," Marie said as she clipped off another thread from the quilt.

"But Marie," Ruth said," If they are successful taking over the western lands it will not be long until they are right here and then hard telling how many of our lands will be claimed by the French and how many of the Indians will join them. I hear the French Canadians have enlisted the help of the Indians while they are fighting. They are probably thinking it will make their country of Canada stronger." Everyone continued working on the quilts while Star was continuing with her preparations to leave. Their quilting bees had provided quilts for wedding gifts, missionaries and those people who needed to know someone cared for them in either sickness or grief. Their favorite was the Bluebird of Happiness quilt that had been a blessing to so many people. The children all came too and learned to play together and to develop their own God-given skills. Star had her latest baby ready to go home. He was so tiny and fit into Star's cradleboard so well. Marie's youngest was seven years old already. Daniel was a big help around the house and also with helping John after a day of building. She knew George probably would be involved in this war and she dreaded it. Marie was so glad her children could be raised here in Georgia. Her jail time in England still had memories for her that time didn't seem to heal. John said he very rarely thought about his suffering there but he was so grateful he came to this great colony of Georgia and was occupied in building a city when he wasn't off to war again. Time really does fly. Marie was folding up the quilt to be worked on at the next meeting. They would get out the quilting frame next time. The quilt was all put together but they had to quilt it yet. No one had room enough for the quilt frame to stay up all the time. Marie just made room for it and the ladies came in when they had the time to quilt on it. She would probably do the most quilting on it but each lady did help even though some of them were taking too large stitches but Marie scolded herself for even thinking that. After all, they did the best they could and maybe they could find fault with her work also.

Marie looked up to see Star all set to go with her family. Marie always admired the way Star could train all her children ready to help her at any time. Star turned to Marie, her dear friend as she prepared to leave. "I am ready to go, Marie. Thank you for having us. The children had so much fun. Rebecca can read so well to them. I was so glad to get this quilt put together for quilting. I guess it will go to our new Pastor," she said as she adjusted the baby. "I really think we will like him, Marie. He promised to come to speak to our Creek tribe. You all would be so welcome too," She said as she looked around at all her English friends. "I suppose he will speak in our language but although some of you know some of the words I know you would be more comfortable in English. He will speak some words in English but you know," she said as she paused and observed all her good friends. "Our language just cannot be translated and mean as much to us for some of the words. They just are so beautiful spoken in our language…well, I guess I better go…. you know none of our tribe would cause you any harm. You have been so good to us."

As she picked up her basket, Marie put some of her delicious corn bread into it. Star was a good friend. She and John appreciated her so much as well as her husband, Bright Arrow. It grieved Star and Bright Arrow that Indian tribes were joining up with the French armies to take over their land—land that belonged to England. Where would it all end? There were rumors of scalping and killing and the ladies wondered how this would affect their families. War had not been declared between France and England but it looked like the Indians would be helping the French to take away their land and then of course there would be an all out war between France and England. Alice knew one of the girls who had been captured by an Indian and everyone was worried that she had been scalped. The French were paying money for scalps. Star was concerned about her tribe too. She knew the other Indian tribes were upset because the Creeks didn't care to join their conflict. It had helped to keep working on the quilt while they were conversing about this news. "Star, I have put some corn bread in to take home with you. Here's some honey too. I know the children will love it for their dinner tonight." Marie put the food in star's basket. "My, my you are really loaded down. Why don't you wait for Bright Arrow, Star? The men should be done with their work soon."

As Star left the ladies wondered how Star managed with such a large family. "Marie, maybe we should get the pattern for the cradle board Star was using. I don't think she could have carried all the different things she had without the cradle board. Of course, her children were helping her carry also." Marie was helping the ladies gather their materials when she paused to talk to Alice.

"She uses that, Alice wherever she goes. When she is working outside she hangs it on a tree limb. I don't think I will ever need anything like that again. I think our family is complete. I worry about all this fighting going on between the British and the French. I think the Indians feel that they will get back their land if they help in this conflict. I know it worries Star hearing her people plotting against her English friends."

Ruth was concerned about their conversation and the effect it would have on Bright Arrow. She tied off her last stitch on the quilt for the day and looking at Marie, she said,"I hope we didn't hurt Star's feelings with our talk about the Indians, Marie. She should know we trust her and her tribe. They have been so good to us from the time we arrived here."

"I don't think she would ever doubt our love for her, Ruth," Alice said. We will have to watch what we say though next time. It is just terrible what some of these tribes do such as scalping and all kinds of savage things. Then I hear that the French encourage it." Alice would be the last to leave. She would be waiting for Charles to pick her up to go back to their Island home.

The ladies continued discussing this war while gathering up all their quilting equipment. Maxi, Marie's kitten, was walking through all their material and thread. He could really be a nuisance at times.

Becky came in and picked up Maxi. Every time one of Maxi and Carmel's litters were born, they always kept one and gave the others away. "I'll be right back, Mother," Becky said. We were wondering where Maxi went. I suppose he was just tired of all the petting and attention he was getting. I don't know where Carmel went."

You could hear Maxi purring as Becky continued out the door. Ruth smiled as she watched the children gathered around their supposedly lost kitten. She knew Maxi would be glad when all the children returned home. The ladies returned to their original conversation. "I guess there is some good coming from it too," Ruth said as she continued getting ready to go back to her home. "Our men are learning how to fight and protect our property. They have been so busy building all these years that they didn't have much time to learn how to protect our city. It gets so lonesome here when they are gone. Ted will be back soon though, because it is about time for him to put in the crops. I know he intends to go right out again as soon as he has the planting done. I will be glad when they all get home to put in their crops for this year."

"That will be great when we have fresh sweet corn again," Marie said. "Here, Ruth-don't forget this. I made extra corn bread for each of you to take home," and she put it into Ruth's basket. Ruth and Marie had known each other for 22 years now. She was one of Marie's dearest friends. Ruth and Ted didn't have as large a family as all her friends. They were just praising the Lord for the two children God had given them.

The ladies were soon gone and Marie had a chance to rest awhile before starting dinner. She wished this war was over but she knew the men needed to protect their property. If only the Indians hadn't joined in with the French troops she knew it would have been over. It was just frightening thinking about all the raids the Indians had made on the villages near here. Star was so sorry some of the Indian tribes had resorted to the barbaric practice of taking scalps from the settlements that were in the way of the French defeating the English armies. She was glad George agreed with John and stayed at home to work here. He was eighteen but they needed him here. He kept telling his parents that so many of his friends had gone but John and she had agreed they didn't want their son anywhere near the army. It was so dangerous. They were aware that some of the men brought their young sons along to carry water and odd jobs around the camp but they had decided against letting George go. They were glad Star's Indian tribe had not joined up with the French.

Rebecca had been outside caring for the children that were playing as the ladies were sewing on their quilt. "Mother," she said, as she came in the house, "Everyone went home now. I think we played every game we knew and read all the stories we have. It was fun for them to have girls to play with. Brothers are alright but… well…you know, Mother, they like to bother the girls when they are playing with dolls instead of going to play their own games. It was fun reading to them. I know it will be fun to be a teacher." Rebecca's black hair was shining in the sunlight. Rebecca was a beautiful young lady. Marie laughed, "Oh, Becky you always loved playing with George as I remember. I would have been glad to have a brother when I was growing up. My mother…your grandma couldn't have anymore children. Besides, honey, you always loved to play with your friend, Wesley too."

"Oh, Mother," Becky said as she blushed at her mother's teasing, "He is different.. almost like family."

Marie smiled as Becky went out to bring her dolls into the house….dolls that she never played with now. She was past dolls but they came in handy to entertain her little guests. She still enjoyed dressing them and even making little clothes for her dollies to wear. Her Papa had even made her a doll house which was frowned upon by a lot of their friends. They wondered at parents who spoiled their children. Marie was not very much older when her best friend's dad was put into debtor's jail. The family lost their home and the children were put into relatives homes. Marie was so glad that Becky would never have to worry about that. Of course, she did need to be concerned about the other Indian tribes coming around the English communities. Rebecca was a blessing to John and to Marie. They didn't know what they would do without her. Rebecca had already started her Hope Chest. Her embroidered things were so neatly done. Marie hoped she would not need to use them soon. She wanted to keep her home a little longer.

"Thank you, Becky, for all your work with the children. I know you would make a good teacher. We need to start the dinner now. George will be in soon from helping with the work on the Peach's home. John and Daniel need to come in to clean up," Marie said as she lifted down the pewter ware from her dish closet. I still have some cornbread left and we have a lot of that ham so with some potatoes it will make a nice meal." Rebecca started setting the table and continued to converse with her mother about the men that were still fighting the war. "I guess Papa will be back soon, don't you think, Mother?" Marie knew Rebecca was interested in seeing John again but she surmised she was just interested in seeing Wesley. Wesley's parents had agreed to send him to help fight against the French. So many of the women were following their men into battle and Rebecca wanted to go along too. Marie had asked John to let her go and leave Rebecca with the chores of the house but he didn't want either of them to follow him. How she missed John when all these decisions had to be made for the children and the farm. She hoped this war with France would be over soon and all the men would be home again.

Soon everyone was seated around the table. George was taking over some of commitments from his father. They all bowed their heads as George asked the blessing on the food. Marie was so proud of George, helping the men with the work in his father's place. Louise Peach was telling her how grateful they were for their son's workmanship. Marie knew Louise would be proud of her home out in the country. More people were building outside of the town and living on plantations.

"Please pass the ham, Mother," George said as he helped himself to the beans and passed them along to Rebecca. "The Peach family was out today to see the progress on their new home. You know, it might not be a bad idea to move out to our farmland. It is beautiful out there in the spring. I even saw a bluebird, Danny. She was sitting on her nest of eggs so we'll be watching to see them hatch." The candles were lit and Marie looked with pride on her beautiful family. John must come back home safely. They needed him with the family. God had blessed their marriage with four beautiful children. Sometimes she looked back on her childhood and their time spent in Debtors jail as a time in another world. They had always been so grateful to Colonel Oglethorpe. How dreadful that her mother had to die in prison. Marie wished Colonel Oglethorpe had come before so that her mother could have been saved.

Everyone was ready for dessert and enjoyed the apple pie she had made earlier that morning before all the ladies came to quilt. "George, we better read the Bible now and pray for Papa and the men fighting in this war. I know he will be home soon to oversee the crops," Marie said as she handed him the Bible. George turned to Psalm 27:1-14 "The Lord is my light and my salvation whom shall I fear? The Lord is the strength of my life of whom shall I be afraid?" You could hear a pin drop as everyone pondered these questions. There was so much to be fearful for and especially when they were missing so many men who were helping the English armies to fight the French. She and John had discussed the idea of moving out to the country and letting George and Mary have the town house when they were married. George would be closer to all his carpenter work and John was inclined to put more time into farming. George would always be there to help at Harvest time and John always stepped in to help George when needed.

It was soon time to go to bed and everyone was tired from their daily chores. It was no time when all the good nights were said and the house was quiet. Marie went to her room and was soon in bed but she went to sleep praying John would soon be back with her and they could resume their life together again. How she loved him…the joy of her life…the father of her children. His faith was an inspiration to her. "Oh, God protect him through the night," she breathed as she fell asleep.

Chapter 6

It was a hot day this July of 1764. Marie was preparing dinner for her children and also the men in the fields. She was so thankful she had this oven made into the fireplace. She knew that some of her friends no longer had to do this kind of work. John still held with the views they started when they came here to Georgia in 1733. There would be no slavery in their colony. Yet slavery was legalized in their beautiful colony in 1750. John said she must realize they couldn't fight it anymore. They could only regulate it in their own home. Maybe if the citizens of Savannah had their freedom taken away in jail as they did they would understand how these niggers felt. It was still humiliating to hear them talked about as ¾ a person. She missed living in town and having her friends drop in often. They had really enjoyed their beautiful home in Johnson Square of Savannah. She felt so isolated out here in the countryside of Savannah but she would probably miss the beauty of nature here in the country if she went back to town. They planned to go back when age prevented them from taking care of their farmland. George and Mary were now living in their town house. Mary was so sweet and their whole family just loved her. They welcomed her into the family. George knew her from childhood but as he went into his teens he became really interested in her. She was Rebecca's friend so he saw a lot of her but her visits were puzzling to Rebecca in the last few years. She seemed more interested in talking to George or playing a game just for the two of them. She was glad it turned out that Mary became her sister in-law as she didn't have sisters…only brothers.

Star came over often to help even when they were not in walking distance to the plantation. She had a horse to ride and even took her spinning wheel along to work on one of her projects. It was a familiar sight to see Star come riding up with her spinning wheel strapped on her horse's back.

Since school was out Rebecca came in as much as possible. She was twenty five now and excited about the work she was doing with the children round about them from the plantations. Rebecca was not married yet. She was till waiting for just the right man. She wanted him to be a Christian first of all and she knew God had the right person for her. She was glad she was here to help her mother. Her mother was 64 now. She was so blessed to have Mother and Papa with her. Mother had told her so many stories of her time in jail and how there are so many things her children took for granted but even today she marveled at the beautiful scenery here on their plantation. Marie never tired of watching the birds especially in the spring. She was so depressed in jail but God had all this ready for her and she wondered what her mother and father enjoyed in Heaven.

Marie knew this was not her home but it was a beautiful foretaste of her heavenly home. She could just imagine what God had prepared for her in heaven.

"Come here, Rebecca," Mother said as she looked out of the window to the nest of their bluebird tenant. "I think she is ready to move out. All the baby birds have flown away. Sometimes they make another nest for a second brood but I really think it is getting too late for that to happen." Marie said as she admired the plumage of brilliant blue. Rebecca never tired of her mother's stories of the different birds flying around their plantation.

"I have told the children all the bird stories you have told me growing up, Mother" she said as she put her arm around Marie's shoulders. She loved her mother so much and realized when she had turned seventeen it brought back so many memories of her mother… memories of affluence where her every need was met to spending all those years in the worse kind of jail you could imagine. She was glad those years of comparing were past now and her mother was looking toward the future for her.

"Sit and rest awhile, Mother, you have been working too hard. I can at least set the table. How many are coming? It certainly will not be as many as you have in harvest time. I can imagine Star will be here. She has really been a faithful friend to you, Mother. I know she has kept other tribes of Indians from raiding here," she said as she continued to set the table. "Maybe John would run out to the field to see how many will be coming. Sometimes Mary just goes out to the field to eat a lunch with George. They really are a happy couple and enjoy so many things together. She just wants to be with George.

I almost feel like I lost a friend but it is really nicer having a sister," she said as she put the last setting of pewter down.

Marie leaned back in her rocker as she put her feet on the new footstool she had received as a birthday gift last month. Marie laughed as she said, "It surely took us all long enough to recognize their love for each other. I know you were hurt by it, dear. You will see that they will not shut you out of their lives. Mary and George both look forward to your visits," she said as she noticed Rebecca smiling.

"I know, Mother. Sometimes I wonder if I did the right thing taking this summer job at the boarding house and staying nights. You have so much work to do…canning and making meals for so many. I just might move to the plantation again so that I can help you. I wonder about you doing so much."

"No, Rebecca," Marie said, as she left her rocker and set the rolls out on the table. "Peggy really needs you to help with the children. She has gone through so much. It seems just as the Treaty of Paris was signed last year, her husband came home wounded and needed a lot of care. Of course she has a friend who helps her at times. Lucy doesn't have children and likes to watch the twins. Peggy told me how much you have taught the children. Peggy needs a lot of time to care for Joe. Anyway, Daniel and John are old enough to help me or even in the fields but they would not do anything if you were here all the time." Marie started dishing up the food. She could hear John talking to the men as they were out in the barnyard at the pump cleaning up to come in for dinner. She hoped everyone would like the chicken dinner she had prepared.

Rebecca went to the door to talk to John about the count to set up for this meal. John told her to set the table for fifteen. Rebecca noticed a couple of her students in the barnyard too. Everyone round about heard about Marie's cooking. During harvest time this was everyone's favorite place to eat. No one took their own lunch here. They all dreaded going to the Smith's household. One day Mrs. Smith had sent her oldest son out to ask if they would like apple dumpling or cherry cobbler for dinner. Everyone took fore granted that she meant for dessert. Imagine their distress to find out it was their meal. Some of them were so weak they couldn't walk back to the fields. Mr. Smith always had a hard time getting enough men to help him. Marie thought there was a time she would have been glad to have that kind of meal. She knew it was hard for these men to realize the lack of food in other parts of the world. Ted came in first. He was always glad to help out on the plantation when needed. He was still working as a carpenter. Marie noticed him as she was arranging the dishes on the table. "How is Ruth today, Ted?

I didn't see her in church yesterday so I assumed she was sick. That flu seems to be hitting everyone."

"Yes, Marie, I hate for Ruth to get anything like this. She has a hard time getting over it and seems like it settles in her chest, making her cough to mid summer. Dr. Kelly wants her to get more rest." Ted took a seat away from the table. "Sure smells good, Marie. We always know we get a good meal here."

Everyone was in soon gathered around the table to eat the delicious chicken meal. Rebecca took care of serving the food. She insisted that her mother sit down at the table to eat. Rebecca enjoyed the times she could help her mother. When Rebecca brought out the apple pie Mother had made she could tell this is just what they were waiting for. All conversation stopped until their pie was served. "Did you all hear the latest trial that England has bestowed upon us?" Rebecca asked as she served each one a piece of the pie, "It is called the Currency Act. We will not be able to use our paper money." Ted seemed startled by this news. "Just what are we supposed to use?"

he asked. Between bites of the delicious pie they all commented on this latest development the King had enacted. "We don't need their armies here," George said. "You should see how our men can fight. We can take care of ourselves. They come in those red Uniforms and the Indians will be able to take over. I don't know how the King can even dare send troops over here to protect us." George finished his pie and would have liked another slice but Rebecca had given them all generous slices. There wasn't any pie left. Everyone left the house to go back to work still discussing the right of England to tax them without representation. They stood at the pump awhile talking about it before they went back to work in the field.

Marie and Rebecca visited while they cleared the table and put everything away. "I guess there will be more women to help you, Mother, when the harvest time comes. I could come to help too. So many of the children need to stay home at that time to help in the fields. I think we will just call for a school Holiday."

"Well, I know I could use your help, honey but I would not want to keep you from helping Peggy. We'll wait and see what happens in the meantime." Marie appreciated her daughter's willingness to help.

"Becky, sit down a few minutes before you go back to town. " Becky looked exhausted so Marie had determined she would send her home and do the dishes herself. "I guess you know the rumors going around about taxes. I guess that is what the men were talking about and then also about paper money. We probably will just use the barter system. No one is willing to pay taxes to England. They seem to think we owe them for fighting here against France. Then, to think that we would need a standing army to protect us is all nonsense. There is talk about quartering the army in our homes. Imagine all the work this will involve for us and even take away our privacy. I know Papa is thinking about this all the time. If our products are all taxed going to England we will not have a profit at all. We have to pay for all the men working for us. Of course, our friends who are helping will be paid by our returning the favor and helping them with their harvest."

'I know, Mother, I have heard all that too but I don't see how they can make us pay for their war. I'm sure it will all work out. You know, I was talking to Ruth Miller but everything that England does is fine with her."

Mother laughed as she fanned herself with the apron she had removed before she sat down with Rebecca. "You should know Aunt Ruth by now Rebecca. She will never speak against the King although she agrees with us that we need our freedom. Uncle Ted stands firm for the King and will not tolerate anyone speaking against him. He will probably be the first one to offer shelter for all the English soldiers. Oh, I know Aunt Ruth would protect us at all costs as we would help them."

"Mother, that was a delicious dinner. I don't know how you do it. I would probably have one dish warm while the other was still cooking. Maybe that is why I am not married yet. We don't know, maybe it isn't God's will for me. I will miss having children for sure but I am blessed to be able to teach all these little ones, and," she said laughingly," some of them not so little. I realize that they have a hard time with taking off for working in the fields." Becky stretched and yawned. "Oh, I must go home, Mother, if you don't need me anymore. I am going to bed early tonight."

Marie noticed Rebecca had looked tired since she came. The French and Indian war was over last year but John had not returned home yet. She knew he was helping the officers transfer or go home. A lot of them needed to get back home to their farms and plantations. "How I miss Papa, Mother. He seemed always to have an answer to my problems. I wish he had listened to reason and let George go instead of him. I know they didn't put him out to fight but still the danger was there. I need to get more sleep because I lay awake worrying about him."

Rebecca put her sunbonnet on ready to leave. Marie walked over to her and put her arms around her. "You know, Becky, that we should leave all our problems with the Lord. You need to get your rest. The Bible tells us to cast all our cares upon Him." Marie loved her daughter so very much. She was so proud of her. It hurt her to see how unhappy she was right now. Of course, she usually recovered quickly and was happy living in God's will."

Rebecca went out the door and waved to her mother. She knew Papa would be coming home soon and Mother would send one of her brothers to give her the good news. She just prayed that he would come home safe and sound. There were so many men that came home wounded or not al all. After all the sacrifices they made to help England, she paid them back with all these laws. Since 1760 it seemed to get worse as their new king ascended the throne. He was only 22 but he had been educated to know how to govern his great country. Everyone said his mother always told him to rule with an iron hand. As Rebecca rode into town on her faithful horse she pondered all these things in her heart.

Peggy was waiting for Rebecca when she arrived at the Inn. She looked completely worn out. Marie knew that trying to take care of the Inn and also her family was getting to be too much for her. She did appreciate Rebecca helping her but she was looking forward to her husband's recovery when he would take care of all the registry for the new arrivals.

Peggy picked up her skirts and ran to Rebecca despite her exhaustion. "I am so glad you are here. I don't know what to do with all the children. There has been so many stopping in to rent the rooms too. Please run upstairs and see if you can get the children to take a nap. I can take care of everything in the morning but it just is more than I can handle in the afternoon. I didn't even get the laundry done this morning."

Rebecca tied her horse to a rail and gave Peggy a hug. "I guess I shouldn't have left you this morning. We all need to take a nap. I am really tired too. Mother did need me there with her." They went inside together as they could bear her children playing. "You know, Peggy, you should realize since you had more than one set of twins you are a busy mother." Rebecca laughed as she went up the stairs. All six children came to Rebecca as she climbed the steps to join them. "Oh, Peggy let me do the laundry this afternoon while the children are taking a nap."

"You are a blessing. Do the laundry if you feel able but otherwise I guess it can go to the morning. I did all the sheets. You can hang them on the line if you have time." Just then a horse drawn wagon came up to the front of the Inn and Peggy rushed out to take care of these customers. Rebecca glanced out the upstairs window to see Frank, Peggy's husband bringing her horse out to the barn. Rebecca prayed silently, "Oh, Please, dear Lord, help Peggy to see all of her husband's good qualities. Help her to understand that he has been injured and not able to do a lot of things around here."

Becky made everyone comfortable on the quilt as they quieted down with a promise that they would have a story before their nap. It wasn't long until they were settled down waiting for their story. Rebecca slipped down beside them. She could see the youngest twins were fighting sleep...rubbing their eyes and trying to stay awake for their story. "Now, we will be really quiet while I tell you about Maxi. Maxi was a kitten when he first met little Johnnie. Johnnie was so downhearted. He had no one to play with. He wanted his mother to play with him but she was too busy. She always told him when he turned 6 years old he could go to school and there would be other children there to play with him. He was only four. One day Papa came in from the field and brought him a little kitten. The kitten followed him all over the house. He was a gray kitten. Johnnie loved him instantly. Maxi would roll on the floor and Johnnie would roll with him. He would lie in the sun and Johnnie would lay with him. He would get close to Johnnie and purr." Rebecca looked at her charges who were all asleep. They would beg her to continue the story when they woke up but for now she closed her eyes to get some sleep. Maybe Peggy would let her bring a kitten to the children from their farm. As she fell asleep, she hoped she could do the laundry in the morning.

Rebecca awakened a half hour later and struggled to get out of her position on the quilt. She didn't want to awaken any of the children and she felt better also after her nap. She hurried downstairs to help Peggy with preparations for supper. Peggy was glad for the help Rebecca gave her.

"I'll peel the potatoes, Peggy," she said as she heard another wagon pull up with customers. "I hope we have enough rooms for tonight. You can always use my bedroom for some of the guests." Peggy was thankful Rebecca was so willing to help.

"I don't think we will need your room, Rebecca," she said as she looked up from the registry book. "The Lady's room is very large and usually there are more women than men in the wagons. In fact some of the men would rather sleep in their wagons to protect their belongings." Peggy hurried out to welcome her quests with instructions about the horses and to point them to their rooms as soon as she had them registered. She was surprised to see Frank out by the barn helping with the horses. Maybe he could snap out of this mood he was in since he came home from the war. She knew she was losing her patience with him but she never lost her love for him. She wondered how many more couples were going through the same thing. Anyway she was glad he was home from that war. They had heard so many terrible news reports from the wounded who came home with their scalps still intact.

"Welcome," Peggy said as the people climbed out of the wagon. "Come inside and I will get you settled in no time." She led them to her desk register.

One lady's baby was crying as she tried to sign her name in the registry. "We are glad to stop at a place to get some rest and food," the passenger said. Peggy held her baby while she registered. "She is so sweet, Mam," she said. "My name is Peggy. We are glad you arrived safely. I know the war is over but there are many of our men not home yet. I have a school teacher, Miss Mason helping me today. She is starting the dinner as we speak." Peggy handed the baby over to the mother. She quieted down but Peggy knew the mother would want to go to her room to take care of the baby. "My husband is just coming in so he will show you the Ladies room and also the Men's for your men-folk."

"My name is Faith, Peggy. We are all tired out and feel dirty with all the wind we have gone through to get here. This seems to be a nice town. You are blessed to be living here." Faith was thinking about all the tragedies they witnessed as they traveled. Right now she wished she had never left New York. All the dusty wagon roads and Indian trails they had to travel on, all the while wondering if they would run into any Indians who were there to harm them. Even though the French and Indian war was over, still there was that constant fear. Fear you tried to hide from your children. Then there was the need to wash clothes and no water for miles in either direction. You had to wait until the trail hit a body of water… streams, creeks or lakes. This would be great to rest here for the day and catch up on their laundry. "I know, Peggy we look a sight with all this dirt on our clothes and also I imagine you wouldn't be able to tell what color my hair is right now. You wouldn't believe my hair is blond, now would you?"

Peggy liked this lady who was very disheartened by her journey. She looked so fragile compared to the usual guest here. The ladies she had seen tended to be strong and even helped their husbands with driving the wagons. This lady was no more than 5 feet if she was that. "We will get you settled in no time, dear and before you know it you will be clean and we will even help with your laundry. We also need to wash tomorrow so we can all do the laundry together."

Frank was leading them up the stairs when they heard the patter of little feet. Faith couldn't believe her eyes when she looked up the stairs to see six little ones looking very much alike. Rebecca ran out of the kitchen to rescue her charges so the guests could go up the stairs. She picked up Martha and Mary while Frank rescued the baby boys, Timmy and Tommy. They had not ventured on the stairs but sat at the top looking down. Frank was laughing as he scooped one up in his arm and Faith's sister picked up the other baby. "Welcome to this house of twins," Frank announced. Everyone was soon settled and they found the beds would meet their needs. Each room had several wash basins with warm water already in them. Faith was glad she and the other ladies could get cleaned up for dinner. They could smell the food cooking and were ready in no time to eat.

Peggy thought again how glad she was that Rebecca was here to help her. She looked pretty with her white apron over her blue dress. The children had brought in enough logwood to make the blue dye for the dress. Blue had always been her favorite color.

They had set up for fifteen quests and every place was taken. They had enough trenchers for the children to eat their food. Their family would eat later. Rebecca took care of the serving and Peggy was dishing up the food in the kitchen.

"I hope you all like chicken and dumplings," Rebecca said as she put down the bowl of potatoes. "Peggy made an apple pie early this afternoon so it will still be a little warm."

"The food is really delicious," Faith said. "I would like to introduce our family as we are eating. We were a part of a wagon train but we didn't want to go as far as Florida as the rest of the group wanted to do. Florida is in the hand of Spain now so we would rather stay here. We might look into staying around here if there is something we can do."

"Just a minute. I will tell the owners and maybe Frank will talk to your husband about the jobs here." She went to the kitchen to tell Peggy the guests would like to talk to them.

Frank and Peggy came to discuss the job situation with their guests and Faith introduced them to their daughter, who looked shy as her name was mentioned. Anne was such a pretty name. She was only 10 years old. Rebecca looked forward to teaching her in September. Robert was 8 and with his red hair looked mischievous but Rebecca knew she could handle him. Faith had her sister with them too and her family. Lora's husband had died in the war. She had her children, Ruth, Ted, and Matthew with her. The other family was no relation to them but wanted to stop at Georgia also. There were six of them but before Faith could introduce them they were finished with their meal and left the table.

Frank talked to Faith's husband, Bob and he seemed really interested in making Savannah their home. Frank told him about all the job opportunities there were in Savannah. There were all kinds of jobs in the trades…Tanning, Shoemaking, Harness making, Metalworking, carpentry and other things. Peggy was glad that Frank was taking an interest in their customers. She was glad also that she was able to run the business while Frank was recovering from his injuries in the war. She could see an improvement today in his attitude as he was helping her get the guests ready for the night.

He never talked about the war or the loss of his arm. Yet it was always in the back of his mind disturbing his sleep. He hoped John would come home safe and without any injuries as he had endured. Marie seemed so sure that God was taking care of her husband.

As everyone took care of their chores and the guests found their beds both in the Tavern and in their wagons, the nighttime was quiet with just a little breeze. Frank tried to assign beds with just two in a bed but he knew there were times when they had to put six in a bed especially for the children. They would all sleep across the bed.

It took two weeks to find a job and to start building their homes. Marie didn't even make it home to help her mother. Peggy needed her with all the washing and cleaning all these guests required. The twins were always getting in the way. Anne helped so much and seemed to enjoy taking care of the twins. Becky found out Anne could read well for her age of 10. She knew she would enjoy teaching the new children coming into their town of Savannah.

Finally some of the guests went to their new homes causing a break in the busy tavern. Becky chose this time to visit her family's plantation. Marie saw her coming down the lane on her horse. Becky leaned over and talked to her horse. "I think Mother knows we are here, Lightning." Marie ran down the lane. Becky dismounted her horse and they threw their arms around each other. "I have missed you so much, Becky but I knew you would come as soon as you could. Oh, Becky, God has really blessed us. Your Papa has just returned home. He is waiting for you. He is very tired but he is not injured."

"Mother, I have prayed for this day. As I watched Frank, it made me so nervous thinking Papa would come home like that. We can just praise the Lord. I hope and pray he will never go out to war again despite his interest in freedom. England will never let us go, Mother. King George III will never back down. May God bless our beautiful colonies." Becky ran down the lane and was greeted by Papa standing on the porch. She had missed him so much. As Marie brought up her horse she could see Becky in Papa's arms. Marie was praising the Lord for his safe return.

Chapter 7

Moving Day....Marie did not think she would ever be willing to move back to town but it was happening now. Their children were afraid Marie and John would be in danger with this threatened war of 1775.

Springtime...Planting time....Time when the bluebirds made their nests for the next brood of little ones. She always liked to think of the Indian legend Star had told them about. The bird was originally a dull color, but due to its gentleness, the gods allowed it to bathe in a sacred lake of incredibly blue water. When the bird emerged, its plumage was a brilliant blue. Star knew now that God made them this beautiful color. Marie saw some in town but nothing like here in the country. She breathed a sigh of acceptance as she turned from the window looking out at the budding tree. Rebecca was just entering the house.

'I've come to help, Mother!" Rebecca said as she saw how exhausted her mother was. "Oh, Mother, you look so tired. I know this move is hard on you but you must realize what terrible times we are in. Every day we pray that God will keep you safe way out here in the country."

Marie just shook her head. "You couldn't imagine what all we have gone through, honey. When we first moved here the Indians were still a threat...Oh, not Star's people but others that would come around here looking for trouble. And they didn't give a second thought to scalping whoever was in their way."

As Marie leaned down to take baby Emily out of her cradleboard, Rebecca noticed how beautiful her mother looked even at the age of 75. She wanted to take care of her parents. As the only daughter Rebecca felt it was her responsibility and honor to help her parents. Her sisters-in –law were so helpful but they had their own parents to help except for Mary whose mother had died during her sister in-law's childhood.

"Now is the time to move, Mother before this threatened war gets to be the real thing. I know they are preparing our military for an all out war. I hope Papa comes back before that happens. I wish we could try to make peace with England. After all, it is our mother country. I know all through my childhood Aunt Ruth is always standing by England. You would think that she had never gone through the trials you and Papa have gone through. I guess she just judges England by how good Colonel Oglethorpe was to everyone when Savannah was first settled."

Marie smiled as she looked down at baby Emily with her black curls coming down over her ears, .reminding her of Becky as a baby. How time does fly. It seemed like yesterday when they were living in town and George was striving to build with blocks to be like his Daddy and Rebecca was playing with her dolls. "I guess I will see you more, won't I, my darling baby granddaughter. We will be living in town with you." It didn't seem like she was already nine months old. Turning to her daughter, she said, "getting back to their conversation, "Ted has been quartering the troops in their home ever since the Quartering Act was passed in England in 1765. He just counts it a privilege to help out England in any way they can and Ruth never says anything about it. She goes along with whatever Ted wants to do." Becky put Emily down on the floor.

Emily was crawling around, getting into anything she could find. "I hope we can get something done, Mother, with watching Emily." She laughed as she picked up her daughter. "I know Mary has about everything packed up to move here. I left John and David with her and also Pricella, of course. She is old enough to help Mary with them. They all love it when they can stay with Aunt Mary. Mary is so good with all the children. George wants to come back here. He thinks it will be easier to help Papa with the field work. I know Papa would rather be tending to his carpentry work than working in the fields even though I wonder about him working full time at his age. Here, Mother, let me take this barrel to pack your dishes. Are you taking all your furniture?"

Marie looked longingly at all the furniture John had made for them. She supposed that Mary could use some of it when she came to live there but Marie felt that she needed to have it herself. "There will be enough room in the wagon to move all of it, Becky. Mary has her own furniture and if she needs more living here, I know George can make anything she would want."

Marie could see this was really bothering her mother. Papa had agreed it would be good to move into town but Mother was having second thoughts about moving. "Oh, Mother, we just want to do what is best for you. You have done so much for us. We would never be able to do as much for you. Let's leave the furniture and pack up the other things," she said as she removed the dishes from the dresser. Marie joined her daughter in packing up their dishes.

"And what is Wesley doing this morning, Becky?"

"He is still at the Smith's home, Mom, doing some remodeling. You know Louise is expecting another baby and they need more room," she said as she put another pewter dish in the barrel. "It seems like a miracle yet, Mother, that I am married and have this family. You always teased me about Wesley but you know I only thought of him as a friend until he came back from the last war. He is so good to me and I am really proud of his skill in carpentry.

They were busy all morning and stopped to fix a lunch for George and the men out in the field. They could hear the men gathering at the pump to clean up before they would come into the house to eat. You could hear George's voice above the others and as usual they were discussing the latest war or reconciliation with England. By the time the men came in everything was on the table. Marie had made a stew which had cooked all morning in the kettle over the fire in the fireplace.

"It sure smells good in here, Mother," George said as he came in first with his helpers. "It looks like you have a lot of packing done also...Oh, Becky, I didn't know you were over today."

"I came to help Mother pack, George. Mary is taking care of the boys today. I suppose you were looking for her out in the field," she said, laughing as she set the kettle in the middle of the table along with some of the bread just coming out of the oven. "I know she goes out there with your lunch at times. She told me she loves to be there with you, especially in the beautiful planting time.

The men were all seated now and conversing among themselves. "Did you hear the latest, George?" Andy asked as he helped himself to the delicious stew. "George Washington has accepted Congress's unanimous choice for Commander In chief of the Continental Forces. Sure looks like we are in this war to me."

George bowed his head before answering and everyone prayed as George led them in prayer for John to come home safely and for the good food Marie and Rebecca had prepared for them. "I hope this is the last time Papa will feel he needs to help fight our battles," George said as he served himself with some of the stew. "If this develops in an all - out war against England then I should be the one to go. After all, I am 33 now and Papa has done his duty for our Colony. I pray that Papa will realize that," and he continued eating his dinner.

Marie was sitting with the men, eating as Rebecca was cutting the pie to serve them. She didn't know if she would ever cook and bake as well as her mother. Maybe when they finally moved her parents to town she could take some lessons from her. She was always so interested in teaching school before she was married there was no time to learn to cook. She enjoyed so much teaching her children at home now and looking forward to teaching Emily.

In no time at all the pie was served. Everyone marveled at the delicious dessert Marie always provided for them. George was the first to leave the table. "Let's get going, fellows. We only have a few more acres to hoe the cotton. "

"That's another thing, George," Marie said. "I always look forward to seeing the cotton growing. I think at harvest time of that verse in the Bible about the fields being white unto harvest." George smiled as he turned to his mother.

"Mother, you know Papa will bring you out here anytime you want to come. Then you can see all the (Bluebirds of Happiness} that you always told us about as children," he said laughingly. "Well, come on guys we need to keep going," and everyone headed out to the fields.

Marie cleared the table while Rebecca put Emily down for her nap. Emily was tired from playing and was soon asleep on the blanket Marie had laid down on the floor. Marie sat down in her rocker while Rebecca finished with taking care of Emily.

"Mother, I can stay another couple of hours but then it will be time to go home and make our dinner. Maybe you will feel better about this move when Papa gets home. I would think it was long past time for him to come home. I understand George Washington sent just about everyone home. I suppose he will recall them if a war is declared."

Marie sat down in her rocking chair again as she pushed her hair back from her face. She knew she looked a sight and as she looked around to see barrels ready to pack her household things and a stack of towels folded ready to go she felt discouragement overtaking her spirit. Marie's hair was just as black as when she was young but she knew there were strands of silver scattered throughout. She knew soon it would be time for her heavenly home. In the meantime she would focus on the wonderful life they had in town before moving out to the country. John always said changes seemed to be hard for her. She was looking forward to his safe return home.

Marie sighed as she looked up at her daughter. "Oh, Becky, I don't think there is any solution except a war. King George is not going to let us go. History proves that he would not part from the colonies he feels are England's to do with just what he wishes." Marie's problems seemed overwhelming. She knew that God sees and answers every request we have but when John was gone she could only see death and destruction coming. John always gave her so much encouragement. She couldn't wait to have him home again with her.

Rebecca could see her mother was losing hope. She knew it was the fact that she would be moving out of here soon. If only Papa would get home before she had to move out. "Oh, Mother, I hate to leave you when you feel like this. You know Savannah is so beautiful with all the flowers in bloom and then all the squares are so different than any other town's. You liked it when you were living there. I think the Johnson Square is the prettiest of all...especially in the spring."

Marie leaned her head back on the rocker and faced Becky standing at the door with Emily in her arms. She needed to start back home but she didn't want to leave her mother in such a sad state. "Oh, Becky, I should have known it would be like this. God tells us in the Bible that when you get older your children will lead you around wherever they want you to go."

Becky was exasperated. "Mother...Where is that verse in the Bible? You know we want to take care of you. That's a terrible thing to say. You have so much to be thankful for. I remember all the good times we had as a family. I was ten years old when John was born and then two years later I remember Daniel and how happy we were with all six of us sitting around the table for dinner. We are so glad to have you and Papa for our parents. All our friends loved to come here where they could play and have the cookies you made for them. We love you Mother. Just count it a privilege to watch over you. Please let us do these things for you."

Oh, Becky, I am so sorry for all the stress I give you but I think we can find something in the Bible for all our needs. In John 21:18 it says, "Verily, verily, I say unto thee, when thou wast young, thou girdedst thyself, and walkest whither thou wouldest; but when thou shalt be old thou shalt stretch forth thy hands, and another shall gird thee, and carry thee whither thou wouldest not." Honey, I am so sorry but I know I am getting old so I will just have to adjust to the circumstances around me. I wish your father would come home. He has served enough in these wars. I must let you go. I will be fine, Becky. It sometimes comes over me. I guess it is when I am tired and have not kept my eyes upon Jesus."

Emily was starting to squirm and wanted her mother to let her down. "I must be going, Mother. I know you keep busy here and that is good for you. My…how many quilts I packed today. It would take me ages to make all of those. I know Papa will be home soon," she said as she proceeded out of the door. She had taken the buggy today and George had the horse all set to go. Marie followed her outside, hugging Becky as she picked up the reins to go home. "Wait, Mother, I hear a horse coming down the lane." Marie looked down the long tree lined lane discovering John riding up, she was all smiles as Becky picked up Emily and stepped down from the buggy. Papa had arrived home at last.

Marie ran down the lane to meet him. John could hardly wait to hold Marie in his arms again. How he missed her and of course the whole family. John got off the horse and in no time had Marie in his arms. Rebecca stood back as her parents greeted each other. She was so proud of them and realized the strength of their love and their trust in each other. She knew God had first place in their hearts but as they reached up together for God in thankfulness they became closer to each other. John turned then to his daughter and granddaughter. John took Emily in his arms, so thankful that he still had his arms and his legs but these were his family he was fighting for. He wanted them to enjoy peace in this new land and not have England in charge of their country.

John had the horse reins over his arm as he walked the rest of the way up the lane with Emily in his arms. "I am leaving, Papa. I am so glad you are home. It makes it easier to leave Mother. This move is making her so upset. I will see if everyone can come over tomorrow for dinner. I know you have a lot of things to tell us. I think, Papa, that your hair is just as red as ever. It is so good to see you again. I just thank God for his care for you. We all love you so much."

"Becky, I have a few gray hairs and I know it will be more as time goes on. You better get home to your family. That will be great if we can all get together tomorrow. Where are those grandchildren of mine, Becky? I miss seeing John and David here and Pricilla too, of course. They make life interesting."

"Interesting is putting it mildly, Papa, I knew Mother and I would not get anything done if I took them with us. Anyway, they will be having a good time with Mary and the children.

"Mother and I always laugh at the times you left them with us and they ate dinner with us. Remember, Marie when they would fight over who was going to serve the dessert? Laughingly, he said, "We solved that one. They took turns. We always said even when you were all growing up that you couldn't get better entertainment in the whole city of Savannah."

"Wesley and I are so glad you enjoy the children, Papa and now it is time for you to stop this helping in the war and stay home with Mother in the city of Savannah. Please don't go again, Papa," and she took Emily from his arms.

Becky hurried to her buggy and climbed in happy to be going home without all the worries about Mother. Papa would take care of her. She was sure they would all remember mother's verse in John. They wanted them to just let the family help. Praise God for letting her belong to such a caring family.

Papa and Mother stood waving as Becky left. They stood there until she was out of sight. John put his arm around Marie as they walked to the yard. Lightning trotted along with them.

"Well, I will put this horse in the barn and then I will be in honey. Fields look good. I am sure the boys have been working hard."

"I will warm up some food for you, John. I know you must be starving."

"I certainly am. I didn't want to stop when I was so close to home. I kept thinking I didn't know how much news you heard here at home and I was afraid you had already heard about the trouble at Lexington. I guess we will have to admit it. We are in this war and I don't see how anything can stop it. I was there, Marie. Eight of my friends gave their lives and ten were wounded. I keep remembering them but…My.…It feels good to be home," he said as he went on to the barn and Marie went into the house. She remained silent through the conversation but she knew they would discuss it more when John came in. She had to convince him that his time of military service was over. She knew it would be so hard for him to give it up.

Chapter 8

Marie struggled to get out of bed this early summer morning of 1775. It had taken a couple of months before she finally yielded to going back to her old home. She knew she wouldn't get used to living in town again. Yet she knew it was for the best. John was already downstairs eating his breakfast. He wanted her to get a little more sleep this morning. She could hear Rebecca's voice so Marie knew she had come over to help them get settled to their townhouse. Marie didn't want to take up Rebecca's time by keeping her waiting. She led a busy life with taking care of her own family and helping out at the Ordinary at times. It was interesting to hear about all the different people who traveled and stopped at the Ordinary for food and lodging. Rebecca had missed her Papa so much when he took time from his duties at home to help George Washington. It was getting to look like an all out war more and more. Congress had already dispatched Washington to command the Army. By rights John felt like he should be there as well.

He was in his 70's now and couldn't really endure army life. Besides it would soon be harvest time and George had raised a big crop this year and would need his help out on the Plantation. He was so glad his children had convinced Marie that she should come to town to live. He didn't want her all by herself out in the country. They had been given a small piece of land in the country as everyone else had along with the first settlers in Georgia. They bought other land to go with their property. It was time to let George farm the land and time for John to continue on with his carpentry work mostly making furniture for the residents.

Marie was having trouble getting out of bed with cramping and stiffness in her legs. She painfully left her bed as Maxi jumped up to greet her. She quickly sat down again and picked up the purring kitty. He was a friendly pet and it brought memories back of the first kitty they had. This was just one of the many Maxi's Marie and John had been blessed with throughout their married life. It was one of the many good things that had come about as a result of their trials at the Debtors Prison in London, England. She was on the side of the bed, considering the reason for being here instead of at their beautiful country home. Mary and George were living there now. She knew they would enjoy it just as Marie and John had loved the country living.

Marie's hair was streaked with silver now. In fact, it was more silver than black at this point. It was a blessing to live so close to all their children. She remembered also how hard it was to leave the country for their townhouse. Of course, she knew God wanted them to move here. She knew as the Bible said that when you get old your children take charge of your life. "I need to go downstairs and help Rebecca," she said aloud as she started walking down the stairs.

"There you are, Mother," Rebecca said as she looked up the stairs at her mother coming down. "How are you feeling today? We have been concerned about you. We thought yesterday might have been too hard for you with your rheumatism."

Rebecca was 37 now and busy with her family. "I need to get back home, Mother. I have your breakfast on the table. Here, let me help you," she said as she led Marie down the remaining stairs. "Papa is waiting for you. I left the children sleeping and I really need to get back home. We need to get your bedroom downstairs. This is too hard for you."

Rebecca was concerned about her mother's health. It had taken a few months to convince her to move to town. Rebecca knew she couldn't continue to make their meals as she had chores to do at home. She hoped Marie would start to feel up to taking care of her own home. It hurt to see her mother in such pain but she knew the pain was worse in the winter. She watched as Marie went over to John first to wish him good morning with a kiss and such a sweet smile. She was thankful for God's leading through their life. What a blessing to have such loving parents. Marie sat down to the breakfast Rebecca had made for her.

"Mother, I can come back this afternoon. I need to make breakfast for Pricella and James and also Emily now. She eats food from the table. I just mash everything up and she can eat it. I think she does better than the older ones at times," she said laughing as she went to the door, and Papa don't worry about this war. There are younger men who can go," she said as she opened the door.

John turned to his wife when their daughter left. "Marie, this brings my mind back to when we first came here…just the two of us. This is great eating breakfast with you." John leaned over to take her hand and together they praised God for their children and for their home. John could see Marie had aged but she was more beautiful than ever. Everyone had always told them how striking they looked together with his hair so red and her hair so black. Now it was time to accept their age and enjoy their remaining years in this town of Savannah. "John, I am always happy when you are here. I guess it doesn't make any difference where we live as long as we are together. I missed you so much while you were away. Do you think this will be an all-out war with England?"

"I know Congress must pass the Declaration of Independence and we don't know how the King will respond. Congress already declared that we are in a state of defense. They did that in May, and then in June they appointed George Washington as General and Commander-in-Chief of the Continental Army. I've worked with him, Marie, and I know he will be a good commander. He depends on God to lead him in the right decisions and you should just see him on that white horse of his."

John finished his breakfast and silently thanked God for his beautiful wife. Marie glanced up as she finished her tea in wonder again over God's faithfulness and love in bringing them together to live in this beautiful country when everything looked so bleak to their young hearts in England. She saw still the same twinkle in his eyes that had caught her heart as a young girl.

"I know, Marie, you are concerned that our son will have to go to war. I am concerned as well but we need to accept God's will for them." He could see tears in Marie's eyes as she continued to eat her breakfast. "Right now our sons are busy in the fields but I plan on staying here to help us get settled. I may make a few more pieces of furniture too. I know you left some of ours for George and Mary. You need another dresser for the kitchen and a wardrobe for our bedroom. I will get started on that today while you put your linens away and unpack some of the other barrels."

"Yes, you know I feel so much better with you here, dear, that I don't even need Rebecca to help me today. She can spend the day getting caught up with her own work. I'll get dressed and put some things away. After lunch maybe we can walk over to Ruth's house and visit with her and Ted awhile. I know they don't agree with us about this war but we will protect them if our soldiers take over Savannah. We have made that agreement with them and I know they would do the same with us if the British overtake us. I guess to get right down to it we are under British rule right now but we know that can change soon."

"We are a royal state but that doesn't mean England rules us now anymore than before all this trouble started, Marie. Everything will be the same as always," John said as he moved away from the table.

Marie went up the stairs to change from her gown to her day dress and an apron. It was wonderful to have John home again. She felt as if she had caused her children more trouble than necessary. As she dressed she could hear the voice she loved so well singing as usual. What a wonderful husband he had been to her all these years. She kept her shift on as always but chose a blue dress to wear over it. John always liked her in blue. She wore her apron to continue with her unpacking so that she would keep her dress clean and could wear it over to Ruth's house.

Marie could hear John out in the carriage house ….probably picking out just the right wood for making the furniture they needed. From his singing she could tell that he was enjoying the day at his home instead of being out with the army. She knew George Washington was sacrificing much by being away from his home in Mount Vernon. Marie thought maybe it wouldn't come to a war and hoped there would be an agreement with England instead to prevent that from happening. Marie was busy putting away the linens when John came back to the house.

"I think we will have two of our sons here for dinner today, Dear. Daniel and John wanted to come by and talk to us. I think I know what they are planning. I have been against our sons going to war before but I guess I will not have much to say about it this time. After all, John is 31 now and Daniel is 27. I was able to keep all of them from serving in the French and Indian War but now I will not be able to go myself and of course they are at an age now to make decisions for themselves. In fact, I was thinking of going back after the harvest but the more I think about it I have more or less decided to forget about it."

Marie was heartbroken to hear this news about John and Daniel. It seemed like yesterday that they were playing with the blocks John had made for them and enjoying the friends that came by to play. "Oh, John how terrible this will be for their wives. You know, they are both expecting babies. We will soon have two more grandchildren. God has blessed us so much, John. Well, all we can do is pray about this but I am so glad you have decided to stay home this time," she said as she cleared out another barrel.

"I am sure Rachel and Johanna will do fine while they are gone, Marie. We will help them all we can. Why don't you put that away for now and we will go over to see Ruth and Ted. Well, maybe we should eat our meal first here. Just warm up some of that soup Becky brought over this morning."

Marie quickly warmed up the soup and as she and John sat down to eat, she noticed how tired he looked. He needed this time to relax and enjoy his family.

"How thankful we are for this food, Dear Lord," John prayed, "These are trying times and we need to depend on you for our every move. Please give us peace that we may live in this beautiful land in freedom and tranquility. Change the heart of our King and let him understand that we are a separate country and ready to defend ourselves. Protect our children from all harm and we will give you our thanks and our love. In Jesus name, Amen."

John took up his spoon to taste the delicious soup. "Well, Marie I think that you have taught our daughter well. Except for your own soup, I don't think I have ever tasted anything so good."

"John, I am so grateful for all your encouragement through these years. Ruth tells me Ted never says anything about how the food she prepares tastes…just that if he eats it, she can assume that everything was fine."

"Well," John smiled, "I know how much Ted loves and admires Ruth. I guess it is just his way. If everyone was alike I guess it would be a dull world."

It was past 1 o'clock in the afternoon by the time they were ready to visit Ruth and Ted. It was often that Marie would notice soldiers coming out of their home. They passed a Red Coat as they entered the house. Ruth and Ted were happy for their visit.

"That is just part of the Quartering Act, John," Ted said as he welcomed them into their home. "We decided there was no use fighting it. You know we are loyal to our King but we can see your side of this issue also and maybe it is time to have our freedom. We hope King George will let us go without any fighting. It is funny but Ruth and I were talking how it makes you think about how God led Pharaoh into letting the children of Israel go to their promised land. We aren't as bad off as that but there are similarities," he said as he headed into their kitchen, "come, sit down. We were about to eat our dessert and there is plenty for you both. Ruth made this pound cake and I don't know how she expected the two of us would eat all this."

Ruth smiled as she cut the four slices to treat their good friends. "We never know, Ted, how many military men we will have to feed and remember ….it probably would get back to the King if we didn't treat them with the utmost care."

Marie and John couldn't get over how good the cake tasted. "I know," Marie said, "This cake takes a pound of butter and eight eggs. Your chickens must be doing very well, Ruth."

"They really are, Marie. I don't know when they have done so well. I guess we are blessed so that we can serve the soldiers just what they need," she said as she poured them another cup of tea. That was another thing. Marie wondered how Ruth was getting so much tea. No one was serving tea anymore.

"Remember, John," Ted said as he enjoyed his cake, "Hedging still stands. We will not dessert you in your time of need."

"It might just be the other way around, Ted. The British are not in command of Savannah yet and we have made a lot of plans for our freedom. But thanks anyway for your friendship and your willingness to hedge for us as we would do for you."

They continued in conversing and reminiscing until Marie and John decided to go for a walk around the square. "It is so good to have you here to live, Marie," Ruth said as they walked their friends to the door.

Marie took John's arm as they walked home. For awhile they walked in silence and all was quiet except for the swish of Marie's long dress. They came upon a group of boys playing marbles and it brought back so many memories of the times they had with their children. Several children were playing tag. The running children and the laughter filled their hearts with joy. "Look, John, there is our church where we were married. Looks different now, doesn't it? Why does everything have to change? Look at the beauty of the flowers and the trees. The azaleas are still blooming and I just love the live oaks with the draping of the Spanish moss. Everything is beautiful, isn't it, honey?"

""It is truly beautiful just as Colonel Oglethorpe told us in the beginning. It is what we will be fighting for, Dear. We probably should amber on toward home though. All our children will be there soon."

Marie stopped. "What do you mean? All our children? I thought just Daniel and John were coming so that they could speak to us about the war. It better not be all of them, John. I haven't prepared anything for our evening meal yet. I can see by the sparkle in your eyes that they are all truly coming. What will I do?"

"Calm down, Marie. Each of them is bringing something for the meal. Everything has been taken care of. You will enjoy their visit. They told me not to tell you too soon. They don't want you to have anything to do for the meal. Let them do this for us." As Marie looked into his eyes...Irish eyes that were smiling, she couldn't help thinking about the wonder of their life together. She took his arm and continued down the cobblestone walk. Everything brought back so many memories, good and bad...like the time her father passed away just when she was so happy he could live to see his grandson, George. How George would love his grandpa to come and wait to be picked up by him. But then she had the memories of her children when they were married and walking up the aisle of the same church their parents had used for their wedding. "Please, God let me think about the good memories and not cause my children any grief with my outlook on life." She knew this came from how spoiled she was growing up and receiving everything she wanted of her parents.

As they finished their walk Marie knew she needed to take a nap before the family came. As she went up the stairs, she turned to John who stood at the foot of the stairs. "I will go up to take a nap, Dear. I know you will want to start on your projects," she said as he turned to go outside again. It would be so good to see them all. She wondered if John realized there would be 16 of them if everyone came. They had started their family so late in life that she doubted if they would ever have the experience of being great grandparents. They truly enjoyed being grandparents though. Their oldest, Anne, was so precious.

Marie remembered the first time she discovered Anne's artistic ability. She was showing her the bluebirds in the nest and looking around found Anne sketching the bluebird sitting on her eggs in the nest. The bluebird looked like it could pop right off the paper into her hand. All of their grandchildren were so interesting. She proceeded to remove her dress and lay down with only her shift. She went to sleep thanking God for her dear family.

It seemed no time before she was awakened by the sound of children playing downstairs and the voices of their parents telling them that Grandma was sleeping. Oh, how her mother would have enjoyed seeing her grandchildren, Marie thought but then she gained comfort knowing her parents were waiting for her in heaven. She quickly put on her blue dress and hurried to the stairs to greet her family.

"This is so nice, having you all here," she said from the top of the stairs. "Rachel and Johanna," Marie exclaimed as she slowly went down the stairs. "Thank you so much for coming. I know you aren't going out in public anymore. You both look beautiful to me." As she reached the bottom of the stairs they were the first ones she hugged. Their family was growing and everyone was having a good time.

The men were all gathered around the table expressing their views about the war. "Come girls, lets go over here to sit where there is a breeze coming in." +Johanna, Rachel and Mary all followed their beloved mother-in-law to the living area with the breeze coming in through the window until they decided it was time to finish their dinner preparations. Mary was stirring the pudding and Anne was helping to set the table, shooing the men back away from the conversation place as the other ladies continued to talk.

"Come here, Mary, while I tell you my plan. I think this would be a nice way to send the men off," she said as Mary came to take her place with the ladies. "I have noticed Anne's gift in sketching pictures. When she was much younger she would sketch the blue bird and also Maxi. I couldn't believe it the first time I noticed her drawings. I thought it would be nice if she would sketch each of our families. I have already talked to her and she said she could make a beginning likeness and then later on she could fill it all in and give each of you a copy of your family. With John and Daniel going off to war it would be a nice remembrance and maybe later on she could make a copy for them to take with them."

"That is a great idea, Mother," Mary said. "I know Anne will do it well. George and I always wonder from whom she inherited this talent. It has been a blessing to us."

The men agreed it would be a good idea also. "Let's eat first," Papa said. "I'm too hungry to sit for a portrait. Everyone laughed and they all sat down to a delicious dinner and taste of everyone's offering of food. All you could hear after the blessing was the clang of the pewter dishes being passed around the table.

It was just heavenly to hear all their voices but soon everyone had finished their dessert and it was time to set up for Anne to do the sketching. Anne was only 16 now but already helping out with the school children and looking forward to having her own class one day. A lot of parents hired teachers to come to their homes to teach their children and often would include other children from nearby homes. Anne was hoping for a teaching position in one of those homes.

"Now, I think we should sketch Grandpa and Grandma first. Grandma picked out the place in the house to do the sketches. She wanted it to be in front of the Sampler that Marian did for her Christmas present last year. It shows a picture of the plantation and the beautiful live Oaks that line the lane up to the plantation," Anne explained to the group. "I think she did beautifully with it." As usual, Marian did not comment. Her shyness and her embarrassment when anyone complimented her was a cause of concern of her parents. George and Mary wanted her to have as many friends as her brother and sister but she was content to sit by herself and read as well as embroider. They would often find her perfectly contented with her own company. She was a beautiful girl with her red hair and blue eyes. Anne looked up at her grandparents waiting for her to tell them where to sit. "Grandma, I put a chair there for you and Grandpa can stand right behind you."

"I remember when your Grandpa made this chair, Anne. I am glad you included that in the picture." Marie sat down and John stood behind her. Anne was so pleased with the grandparents she had and was so glad Grandpa would be home again.

The ladies started clearing the table after they saw their parents settled for the sketch. Anne would have a lot of work to do on the pictures when she went home. "Papa and Mother, you are next. Virginia, you can sit in the rocking chair and Joshua on one side. I will sketch myself on the other side of Marian. Papa and Mother, you can stand behind Marian. There you are! Doesn't that look good, Grandma?" Marie agreed that it did look good. How thankful Marie and John were for such a beautiful family. Anne knew she couldn't keep them sitting there for too long but she would be able to sketch in the things she missed tomorrow. Joshua was getting fidgety already. "You can move now, Joshua, you can go out to play now," Anne said as she changed the page for a new sketch. "Next will be Rebecca and Wesley with the twins and Emily."

Anne had Pricilla sit in the rocker with Emily on her lap. The twins stood each side of her and Wesley stood in the back of the rocker. This time Anne knew she had to be quick as she saw that mischievous twinkle in James' eyes. How sweet Pricilla looked with her blond hair. You could tell she was Wesley's little girl. The twins' hair matched but their temperaments were entirely different. Anne soon had the outline sketched and knew she could finish the likeness tomorrow. Everyone stood around admiring the family.

John and Rachel were next. "Anne, let John sit in the rocking chair. I will stand behind him and it will hide my condition." She blushed as she pointed this out to Anne. John and Rachel made such a sweet couple. Anne was happy to accommodate Rachel but she thought no one would know she was in the family way yet. She hoped the baby would have the same strawberry blond hair that this couple had.

Daniel and Johanna were next and Johanna decided to sit on the floor beside the chair where Daniel sat. It would make a pretty picture. Daniel's hair was carrot red and Johanna's jet black. It reminded one of John and Marie.

Soon everyone had sat for their portrait and the evening was approaching. Ted came over just before the sun went down with a container of tea. "Brought you over a little tea to end your day here, Marie, with all your family. Ruth and I admire them. It's a pleasure to have them next door. Everyone silently wondered where Ted and Ruth received all this tea. Ted went home soon and the family scrambled to get their things together and return to their homes.

George wanted to get back to the plantation before dark so their family was the first to say good night. Marie always hated to see them go but knew they now had their own homes. They really had a quiet house once everyone left.

It was hard for George to drive the carriage home in the dark. In fact, George usually just gave instructions to the horses to go home and forgot about guiding them. They always returned home safely while he and Mary held hands all the way. Anne was tired and dreaming how she would finish the sketches. Marian and Joshua were worn out and went to sleep in the back seat of the carriage.

Just as they bid good-bye to George and his family Rebecca and Wesley, along with the twins and Emily, crossed the cobblestone roadway to their home. "I'll see you tomorrow, Papa and Mother!" Rebecca called as they walked to their home. It was great to have Rebecca living so close to them. Wesley didn't say anything about going to serve in the army. "Please," Rebecca breathed, "God grant that Wesley will stay at home with his family."

John and Marie stood on the walk with John and Rachel, Daniel and Johanna. "I hope that you both," Marie said to her sons," will wait until your babies arrive before you leave to join up. Your wives need you with them." John and Daniel looked at each other. "We knew you would feel that way, Mother, so we decided early on that we would stay here over Christmas. Our children should be a few months old by then and with your help and their parents it should work out. Anyway, we intend to come back to help George with the crops. It's not like he has slaves to help him although he does hire some of the free Africans around here. We know the war will not be fought in a few months. It will take time for England to see things our way. Hopefully there might still be a peaceful solution…but I know you don't see it that way, Papa," Daniel said.

They bid their parents goodbye and hand in hand with their wives John and Daniel were soon out of sight around the square. As Marie and John went back into the house their hearts were heavy with the quietness of the house and then the rumbles of war. They already had gone through one war - the French and Indian War. One war was enough for a lifetime. Now it would involve their children.

"Here, Dear, I'll make you a cup of tea. We might as well enjoy it as long as Ted brought it over," as he put the kettle on over the fire in the fireplace he laughed. Marie sat down at the table while John made the tea. He soon had it ready and brought it to the table. "If only King George would be more understanding. We tried to show him how serious we were in boycotting their products but he just responded by having the Parliament pass the Intolerable Acts. God grant that he will see reason and work with us for our country's good."

Marie sipped her tea and wondered where this would all end. She prayed that her sons would be safe and that everything would work out well for their beautiful land.

As Marie went up the stairs to bed that night she was so thankful her sons would be staying home until their children were born. John came up soon after. As he pondered in his heart how long his sons would be staying home he knew what they were getting into but there was nothing he could do about it. He slipped into bed beside Marie and thought about all those lonely nights he had spent in his army life. He needed to spend his last years with his precious wife. She had sacrificed so much so that he could serve his country.

The summer went well. They were blessed with good weather and the crops did great. Between the fieldwork and carpentry their sons were kept busy. Several times Daniel and John were tempted to drop everything to help in the conflicts with England. The Congress had already put the colonies in a state of defense on May 10.

It was already July when their whole family was gathered around the table for one of their family meals. Rebecca was passing around the dessert…one of the delicious pies her mother had taught her to make.

"This is really good, Becky," Daniel said as he ate his first piece. "I will really miss this when I am gone in the army. It will be a few months yet," he said as he noticed his mother's distress. "but you all know that since May according to the Congress we have been in a state of defense." Daniel was really more anxious to go than John. He did want to wait until his baby was born but he wanted a free country for this baby and any they might have in the future. He also knew if he didn't go Papa would think it was time for him to join the American troops again.

Chapter 9

It was March of 1776 already. The babies would soon be three months old. Johanna and Daniel's baby had come first and then one week later Rachel and John had their baby girl. Everyone was so happy to have these two little girls…Kathleen and Martha would have some good times together as cousins. Johnanna and Rachel missed their husbands so much even though they had been gone just a little over a month. They heard all the news about the battle pending in Boston and suspected John and Daniel had been involved but were not certain of it. They were hoping that if the British evacuated Boston, John and Daniel would find some way to come home but they knew it would be hard to come into town with so many Tories living here.

John and Marie were confident that Ted and Ruth would protect John and Daniel from all harm even though they didn't understand their friends standing by England all these years. John and Marie never thought it would come to this that they would be the other way around—that they would have to give Ted and Ruth protection against the Patriots.

Marie looked out of the window this early morning to see Johanna and Rachel with their babies. She had asked a few friends over to see the babies. "Here are your grandbabies, Mother," Rachel said as she climbed the steps to the front door. "These little girls are getting heavy. I like the way our squares are with the beautiful parks but it wears you out walking them," she said as she handed Kathleen to Grandma Marie.

Marie couldn't help thinking back to the time she thought she would never have any babies of her own let alone grandbabies. God had richly blessed her and her husband, John. It just taught them when everything looks so impossible and hopeless you need to look up to God who is your strength. She looked with marvel at Martha. "They really are getting heavy, girls," Marie said as she balanced the two in her arms. "Let's get inside and sit down." Rachel and Johanna laughed as they followed their mother-in-law inside her home. She knew Marie could not stand and hold them for very long.

"Did Rebecca get here yet?" Rachel asked as they sat with their mother-in-law. "She thought she would arrive before we did."

"I think she went over to help Peggy check in some arrivals this morning. She should be here soon," Marie said as she rocked the babies. "Peggy has been busy recently. I often wonder if her roomers aren't Tories. I know Peggy and Frank side with us but some of the Tories up north are getting scared of being tarred and feathered. I wonder about so many coming into Savannah. Maybe it is just my imagination though."

Marie looked down lovingly at her granddaughters as she continued to rock them. "When you come right down to it, I do think there are more Tories living here than Patriots. You never hear them talk about it of course but time will tell what side they are on. I believe that if the British army marches in here they will have more friends than enemies."

Discussing the war made Johanna and Rachel nervous. It seemed ages ago that John and Daniel had left for the army. They knew it would be next to impossible for them to get back into Savannah to visit them. They also knew that with God all things are possible.

"Oh, Mother, I think I see Becky walking up to the house. It is so good to see her. I know we live close but it seems we all get so busy we don't have time to get together anymore. We should have our quilting bees again," she said as Rebecca entered the room.

"I am sorry I am so late getting here," Rebecca said as she clapped her hands in glee to see her baby nieces. Rebecca held out her hands to take Kathleen from her mother. "They are really doing well, girls. They look so sweet together. I can just imagine how much fun you have with them! I remember when Pricilla was a baby I couldn't wait until she woke up from her nap. I would admire her and change her before I nursed her. Then when the others were born I wondered why they didn't take longer naps." They couldn't help but laugh at Becky. It was so good to have her for a sister. "Well, Mother, shall I put out the lunch for all the ladies you invited? I will play with these little girls later," she said, handing Kathleen back to Marie.

"There aren't that many coming. Ruth said she would come and Peggy will be here as well. Star will be coming and oh, Charles is bringing Alice in also. I baked some bread and a pie, Rebecca, and then I put some soup in the kettle over the fireplace. We should have plenty to eat serving that but everyone has just one thing in mind-to see these two precious little girls. In fact, right now they are both about asleep. Did you want to lay them down on our bed, or where do you think would be best?"

Rachel jumped up to take Kathleen from Marie's arms. "They get heavier as they sleep Mother. Let's just lay a quilt down here where we can watch them. I brought the baby quilt you made her so I will put that down over here out of the way," and Rachel put her Bluebird of Happiness quilt down, folding the ends over the baby. Johanna put baby Martha down on her quilt next to Kathleen. "I don't know how you managed to make a quilt for both of the babies, Mother. It would take me forever to do something like this."

"I enjoyed doing them, girls. I am so happy to have these grandbabies," she said as she rubbed her arms. "Just not used to holding babies anymore I guess. My arms ache with the rheumatism but I will not give up sharing them or quilting for those I love."

"That reminds me, Mother," Rebecca said as she was setting the table, "We should be doing something for our men in the army. I hear they are having trouble keeping enough socks and blankets to cover them at night. Well, we can talk about that later. Some of our friends think we would be happier under England's rule. I think I hear them coming up the walk now. Warn them not to bother the babies until we have our tea."

Star looked so pretty as she walked up to the door. She seemed never to age. Marie knew she was still helping at the Trading Post and keeping up with her family. She also worked in her church at the Indian village. She still remembered when their Pastor went to start the church for Star and Bright Arrow along with their family and friends.

Ruth came in next, greeting them all and admiring the babies as they slept. Rebecca ran over to give Aunt Ruth a hug. They all felt like Ruth was part of their family. "How are Ted and Gilbert doing, Aunt Ruth? Wesley and I were just remarking that it has been a few weeks since we have seen them around. I suppose they are working on some building project." Rebecca walked back to the table to finish putting on the food.

"They went off on their own a few weeks ago, Becky. I think they might have gone as far as Great Britain. They were talking about seeing more of the world before they settled down. You know neither one of them have taken an interest in any particular girl and that is fine with Ted and I. I just hope they stay out of problem areas," she said as she walked over to the table.

Alice came in as everyone was gathering at the table. "Charles will pick me up again, Marie. He will be visiting with some of the men out at the building site today. I suppose John is helping George at the Plantation but we will be back to visit you both soon. My, it is getting warm already but there was a nice breeze on the boat coming here." Alice joined the others as they all sat down to enjoy their meal. "The bread smells delicious, Marie."

They all came to the conclusion they would like to meet like this more often and take up their quilting again. They were inspired once again looking at the baby quilts. "And I know Star could teach us how to make baskets again. I use every basket we made years ago and would love to make another. How does everyone feel about that?" Everyone quietly asserted, fearing to wake the babies with too much noise.

"Everything is delicious, Marie, as always. I don't get over from the Island very often and this has been a treat," Alice said as she put some of the freshly churned butter on the home-made bread.

"Remember, Marie eating our first meal on the ship coming over here?" I guess they could have served us anything and we would have thought it was a banquet. It is still fresh in my memory after all these years."

'That is why I think we should be so thankful to the King. I know Colonel Oglethorpe urged him to let the people in jail go to America but he was the one who made it all possible. Maybe something will come out of the peace negotiations soon. I know some are fighting a war already but we certainly don't want an all-out war," Ruth said as she sipped her tea.

"I guess we will just let our men folk solve these problems, Aunt Ruth," Becky said as she left the table to look at the babies. "Just look at them. They are awake now. Who wants to hold them first?" she asked as she picked up Kathleen. Ruth quickly picked up Martha.

"Such a beautiful baby, and the way her black curls frame her face is darling, Johanna. My babies had no hair at all. I was despairing of them every having any until they were almost a year old." Ruth passed Martha over to Star and picked up Kathleen. Star gazed at this sweet baby girl. What a privilege to not only know Marie but also to live to see her grandchildren. She knew God did not look on the color of your skin but loved this baby girl anyway even though her skin was white.

"I need to get back home soon. Ted is bringing a few men in for dinner tonight. I suppose I will hear a lot of talk about this war or talk about the "Common Sense" that Paine put out. I enjoyed visiting with ladies for once." Ruth gave Kathleen to Rebecca as she headed for the door. "I will talk to you tomorrow about when you want to meet together, Marie. I will remember this day for a long time," she said as she bid everyone good-bye.

Charles came in to pick up Alice and stayed awhile to talk to the ladies. "It has been a good day. I enjoyed talking to the men but it seems there is a lot of war talk anywhere you go. I could see everything is coming along with their building. I would like to see John, Marie but we will be back in a few weeks. A lot of our projects are completed now and it is easier to get away." Charles was still very husky and tall. Marie always thought Charles and Alice were so attractive together.

"Goodbye, dear friend," Marie said as she gave Alice a hug. They still recalled the days they had met on the ship coming over and what a beautiful relationship it had turned out to be. Rebecca was so pleased with their friendship. It was interesting to be with all these older people who had unusual experiences to recount.

Giving each baby a special hug, Star was the next lady to leave. Star knew it probably wouldn't be as good for their tribe if her friends would win the war that seemed to be starting yet she sided in with Marie anyway. They had lived side by side for years and never run into any trouble. Bidding Marie good-bye she was near tears as she said, "Marie, may it please God to bring us peace and that our children and grandchildren will know each other and live together as we have all these years. May we continue to worship the same God….God who sent His son so that we might have salvation. May God bless you in your home here in Savannah." Marie gave her a hug as she passed through the door.

"God bless you, Star. Thank you for standing with us as we have heard these are times that try men's hearts. I am looking forward to meeting together again and doing quilts. Maybe even knitting things for the army."

"I imagine these babies need to be nursed," Peggy said as she held the two together.

"They have been so good but I can tell they are getting restless now. Imagine waking up from their naps and seeing all these strange ladies. No, Becky, I can hold the two of them. After all, with our sets of twins, I am used to more than one baby at a time. Oh, how precious they are. Take good care of them now," she said as she handed them back to their mothers. "I must leave and get back to registering the new travelers…Of course we aren't getting as many families as usual but we still have the rooms filled most times," she said as she bid them all good-bye on the way out.

The girls sat down to tend to their babies and Becky continued to finish cleaning up after the delicious dinner. "Let's leave soon so Mother can get some rest. This has been a great time to get together.

I'm afraid it might be harder to do this in the future but time will tell."

The babies were soon satisfied and everyone left to go to their homes. Marie went to her bed and sighed with relief as her back relaxed on her mattress. She had a good time but it had tired her out and she was feeling her rheumatism again. She was glad John had finally made room for their bedroom downstairs. She didn't have to climb the stairs anymore.

Marie recovered quickly from the visit and soon the ladies were getting together to quilt and they decided to let everyone follow a task of their choice. The socks they knit would be given to the army but they resolved they wouldn't talk about who would receive the items they made at the get-together in case some were not in accord with the Patriots' cause.

"I don't know where you get all the pretty threads, Star," Marie said. "I guess you have to know just where all the goldenrod, bloodroot and indigo are. I thought I would start out with making socks but I have a lot of pieces left over from the dresses I made for Becky and I also so I will be making some quilts from that material. Some of it would even make nice blankets."

"We don't always have to meet here at your house," Peggy said as she cut off another thread. "I would be glad to have us meet at the Tavern. There isn't very much going on during the afternoon."

"We should establish a time for meeting. I imagine we could even meet at the Church in the Fellowship Hall. I don't think I could get away more than once every two weeks," Becky said as she finished her first block for the quilt. "I think it would be good for Johanna and Rachel to get out some too. I know they get lonely with this war taking their husbands away."

Everyone agreed it would be a good idea and planned to meet again in two weeks. Marie knew she would be working on her socks at home also. She had heard how desperately the boys in the army needed socks besides warm clothing and blankets. Mrs. Washington was knitting socks herself for the army. It was going to be difficult to meet together when all of the ladies were not of the same persuasion. They would have to learn to keep quiet about the war situation.

"Common Sense" had printed a call "Tis Time to Part" and George III concluded a contract with Duke Karl of Brunswick to have 30,000 German mercenaries leased. Hessians would help Britain put down the "rebellious Americans" as King George now called them. American forces were in process at the same time to end the British occupation of Boston, in addition the patriots were now trying to convince the Canadians to join them in the fight. But Canadians didn't want any part of the conflict. Marie pondered all these things in her heart but she knew that man was not in charge God would take care of all these things.

By the first of July there were rumors that a Declaration of Independence had been signed. By August 10 they knew it was true when it was read in Reynolds Square. There were mixed feelings as it was read. Aunt Ruth was sure along with Ted that it was the wrong thing to turn on England in this way. She had been unhappy with Marie and John all along when they encouraged their boys to join the Sons of Liberty. She could see it coming to no good. She remembered the time when the Sons of Liberty raided the British ammunition stores in Savannah and shipped the "liberated" munitions to the Revolutionaries near Boston. Ted and Ruth knew Daniel and John were involved. Now if they were caught, they ran the risk of being tried as traitors. Despite their differences they would always remain friends. The Loyalists were still in the majority and people were flocking to declare their allegiance to the King and to brand those who didn't as traitors. George Washington was in trouble as so many of the troops enlistments had expired. Washington confided in his brother that he thought the game was pretty near up. The discouragement of seeing so many of the men return home was tempered by the battle at Moores Creek in North Carolina where the Patriots were victorious.

There was a sense of celebration at their Christmas mixed with sorrow as they missed Daniel and John. Marie wanted their home fixed up with the usual decorations. John went out to cut down a tree and the children were sitting around stringing popcorn to put on it.

"Where are the candles for the tree, Mother?" Becky asked as she settled the children to popping corn. Martha and Kathleen were crawling around on the floor picking up popcorn that dropped and putting it in their mouths. "Do you think George and Mary will be able to come this evening for our Christmas Eve celebration or will they just come tomorrow for Christmas day, Papa?" Becky asked as she scooped up the two little girls from the floor.

"George said they wouldn't be here until Christmas morning. He doesn't think it is safe to travel out there at night. He told us to go right ahead with our preparations as usual the church is having a service late evening so I thought we would go over there and then open our gifts when we come back here afterwards. We can read the Christmas story tomorrow at dinnertime here at home so that we will all be together. I know George and Mary will want to leave early tomorrow." Everyone was glad that Papa would be here with them for the whole Christmas season. How many times they had celebrated without him.

Marie was relaxing in her rocker while her family was putting the decorations on the tree. Becky was still looking for the candles. They wouldn't light them until dark and then someone would have to watch in case of fire but she wanted to get them out anyway. "Did you say where the candles are kept, Mother?" Becky asked once again.

"I guess I wasn't paying attention, Becky. They are in the third drawer of the kitchen dresser. We never use them until Christmastime so they should be fine for this year. Bring Kathleen and Martha here. I will rock them for awhile and keep them out of your way," she said smiling. It was so good to have them here to enjoy their first Christmas.

It wasn't long until the tree was decorated with all the popcorn and the candles. The candles were put on later when they came home from church. The air was cool as they walked to church but the ladies all had their shawls to wear. The children were hoping for a Christmas snow the next morning. The message was inspiring and the fellowship with their friends encouraging. Everyone had hopes of peace in the coming year…no matter what their persuasion.

Becky, Johanna and Rachel put out all the special treats for their late supper. Papa was overseeing the lighting of the candles. Wesley indicated that he would sit there and eat while they sat at the table. Martha and Kathleen sat in the special seats their Grandpa had made for them. Becky sat beside Wesley to eat. There was so much their family was thankful for.

"It is so beautiful, Wesley, with the candles sparkling in the evening and making shadows on the popcorn and the evergreen tree shines through it all. It is so peaceful in this land of turmoil. How I wish we would have peace here in these beloved colonies of ours. How I love you, darling," she whispered as the others were involved in pulling their chairs around the tree.

Wesley put his arm around Becky," I have always loved you, honey from the time I came over to visit your brothers. I always had you in mind."

Wesley and Becky looked up to find all eyes on them and blushing, Becky said," We were waiting for you all to get settled! We better get this going so we can all get our children home and in their beds." As far as they knew John and Daniel were safe. Marie was so glad to have some of her grandchildren here tonight. Their gifts lay under the tree and they were soon ready to open them. Kathleen and Martha were allowed to open theirs first. Everyone was impressed with the rag dolls Marie had made for them. Marie had dressed the dolls in material left over from Becky's dresses. Kathleen's doll was dressed in blue and Martha's was dressed in pink which reminded everyone of the azaleas that grew in all the squares of Savannah. Rebecca's children were next to open their gifts. Marie had made them each little baskets with embroidered inserts for each one. Maxi wanted to get in on the fun and jumped into one of the baskets. She then jumped up on the harpsichord and from there to Marie's lap.

"She needs to go outdoors, Marie. I don't know what will happen if she decides to jump up on the Christmas tree with all the candles lit." John could see Marie wanted to hold her. "Alright, better watch that tree, Becky," he said as he sat back down to watch the children enjoy their gifts.

Pricella went over to Marie to hug her with thanks for her gift. "I will use it to put my necklace and a few other things that I have made, Grandma and thank you for reading us the Christmas story and just for being here, Grandpa. We have missed you so much. Of course, we miss Uncle John and Uncle Daniel now. Uncle John always kept us laughing," she said as she sat down by her mother.

"Remember, Uncle George and Aunt Mary will be here tomorrow. We will really have a lot around the table then. Aunt Mary is bringing some of her delicious churned butter and also some of the cheese she makes. I don't think Anne will be doing anymore drawings of the families but that was fun, wasn't it?" Marie looked around on all her sleepy family. "I think we better call it a day and meet together again tomorrow."

Rebecca laughed, "Oh, Mother, I think you are the one that is tired but the children are all yawning too so maybe we better all go home. Wesley, you can carry Emily and we will all follow you down the dark walk. It has been wonderful, Mother," she said as she hugged her mother and Papa good-bye. Let us pray we will soon have peace and all be together again."

Marie and John had so much to discuss after they went to bed. They always had so much to talk about throughout their marriage. "It was a beautiful Christmas eve, honey," John said as he gave her another hug and kissed her good night. "We need to go to sleep now or we will never enjoy our Christmas day. I did miss George and Mary with their family here tonight. I didn't give you your gift tonight. I will do that tomorrow, sweetheart."

"I thought you would sing a Christmas carol tonight, John. I missed you singing. Maybe you could do that tomorrow when everyone is here. You are right. We need to go to sleep. I love you so much and am so glad you are home."

Daylight came far too soon for both of them. They remembered the years when if they weren't up by five o'clock they felt they had lost half the day. There had been so much to keep them busy on the Plantation. How rewarding it was to feed the animals, to gather the eggs, to churn the butter and to admire the scenery around about them.

Marie was up first and went to the kitchen to prepare their breakfast. By the time John came out of their bedroom the bacon was done and Marie had the eggs frying. She made tea for this special day of Christmas. "Did you see the snow, John?" I think the children's prayers have been answered. I hope they get up in time because it doesn't last long here in Georgia. Sit down to eat, dear. I will have it ready in a few minutes."

"Let me be the first to wish you "Merry Christmas," Marie. We will pray by this time next year John and Daniel will be home with us. Let us rejoice in the meaning of this day, the day that Jesus was born so that we might have salvation. We could gather around the harpsichord and sing while you play some Christmas songs."

Marie walked over to the table putting their breakfast down and giving John a hug and kiss. "How glad I am that you are home this year. I will give you your gift as soon as we have our breakfast." John knew Marie was making him something as she ran to hide it every time he would come into the house. She made beautiful things and he was anxious to see her gift to him this year. He had something special for her.

They were no more finished with their breakfast than they heard the sound of horses outside. John looked out to see George's family getting out of the wagon. They were soon inside and all rubbing their hands to get warm. "We came early, Papa," George said. "We want to be gone before it gets dark. Just am not sure how things are going with this war. I know it hasn't affected us here in Savannah as it has in the northern colonies but you never know what will happen. The children are so excited to come so we wouldn't miss it for anything."

They were soon all inside and everyone wishing them a Merry Christmas. Marie served them a breakfast and then the children all went outside to play in the snow. They were trying to get enough to make a snow man or snow balls to throw at each other. It was joy to Marie's ears to hear the laughter of the children playing. Soon Rebecca and Wesley came to join in the fun with their children. While they were playing the women worked on the dinner. Mary had brought her delicious cheese and butter. She brought jellies and a pound cake she had made for the occasion. Rebecca had cooked some beans and had some other vegetables to go along with Marie's wild turkey. It was soon time to eat their dinner and the rest of the family to open their gifts before George and Mary had to leave for home.

While they were enjoying their dinner and the fellowship of their family they didn't realize that George Washington and his troops were taking advantage of the German Celebration in Trenton and surprising the Hessians to take Trenton and secure a victory for the Colonies.

"That meal was delicious, Mother," Rebecca said as she picked up Kathleen to finish feeding her. "You can relax for awhile, Rachel. I will take care of this baby girl. She can eat some of these foods that we mash up for her. I will sit on the floor here with her and you can find a seat. We have gifts for George and Mary and their family. We need to do it early so that they can get home." Rebecca took off her apron before she sat down.

John sat down beside Marie. "Children, I think I will give your grandma her gift before we pass out yours. I have been waiting awhile to give her this." The children agreed Grandma should be first. "Here you are, dear. I'm afraid I didn't wrap it very neatly but remember I was thinking of your beautiful blue eyes when I chose to give you this," he said as Marie took off the ribbons that bound the package.

Marie held up a beautiful blue topaz pendant for all to see. Everyone was in awe at this indescribable piece of jewelry. Anne jumped up to see it better. Marie was speechless for awhile. When she recovered she beamed her pleasure and asked John to fasten it around her neck. "I just love it, honey, however did you find such a pretty necklace?" She gave him a quick hug. "I think I saw Star wearing a similar necklace. It was a different setting."

"You're right, Marie. I noticed Star wearing it and thought that stone would look nice on you so I asked Star about it. Young Cornstalk makes these and has a shop over in the Trading Post. I ordered it from Star and she brought it to me while I was working on the Peach's home. I am so glad you like it. I will enjoy seeing you wearing it, dear. It would look nice on your new dress you made when you go to church next Sunday." He gave her another hug and whispered, "Love you."

Marie gave John two pair of hand knitted socks. "It isn't much, John but I thought you needed new ones. You went through so many when you were in the army."

John always liked the socks Marie made ever since he received the first pair on the ship when they came over to Georgia. Anne, Marian and Virginia really liked the baskets their Grandma made for them. Joshua like the carved horse his Grandpa made for him. "Oh, Grandpa," he said. "It looks just like Thunder who we have out at the Plantation! He is just perfect. Thank you so much!"

It was time for George and his family to go back to the Plantation. They went with good feelings in their hearts of God's love, the love of their families and the great time with their cousins. As they all climbed into the wagon, John was thinking about Isaiah 44:3 "I will pour out my Spirit on your offspring and my blessing upon your descendants."

Chapter 10

It was early morning in the fall of 1777 as Marie looked out to see all the beautiful changing leaves on the trees round about. She noticed Ruth out already passing the house. Ruth would be busy today. Ted and Gilbert were home for the weekend. Marie turned to finish cleaning the kitchen from their breakfast. John was out already helping the neighbors down the street with their new shed as the last storm had destroyed their old one. Marie just arrived at the kitchen again when she heard the front door slamming. She was startled by sobs as Rachel entered the room.

Her daughter-in-law's face was streaked with tears and she looked like she had been up all night. "What is wrong, Rachel? Where is Kathleen?"

"Oh, Mother, Mother, you will never believe what has happened. Ted said he saw John led off as prisoner after the battle at Saratoga. It was just before our victory when it looked as if the British would win the battle. Mother, they probably put him on one of those prisoner ships," she sobbed. With her arm around her shoulders, Marie led Rachel over to the nearest chair.

"Now, Now, Rachel, let's not jump to conclusions. You know we have heard rumors after rumors since the boys left. None of them turned out to mean anything. Even if Ted saw the soldiers taking John that doesn't mean that he is still there. Why don't you go down and talk to Papa about it? He has been in so many battles. He will know better how to understand the news. Everyone was so excited that we won that battle at Saratoga. Somehow I know my sons are safe. John is working down the street replacing the Jones shed. Run down, dear and see what he says about this." Marie put her arm around Rachel and led her to the door.

As she ushered Rachel out the door she noticed Ruth coming back from her errand. "Ruth, Ruth, could you come in for a minute? I know you are busy today but this will not take long."

Ruth passed Rachel on the cobblestone walk and greeted her as she went by but Rachel hardly looked at her. Her face was blotched with tears.

"What has happened, Marie?" she asked as she entered the doorway. "Where is Kathleen? Has something happened to that baby girl?"

"Come in and sit down, Ruth. No, nothing has happened to Kathleen. She must have left her with her neighbor. She is in tears because she heard John was taken prisoner. Is that why Ted and Gilbert are home? We heard that our soldiers won that battle. I don't see why the British soldiers would have been able to take any prisoners. I know that if they have taken them to one of those prisoner ships it will be terrible on them." Marie was starting to cry. She knew she could depend on God to take care of her. She thought that living in jail for all those years had taken all the tears she had to shed but this was just too tragic to hear. Maybe John would have some answers. She hoped Rachel would come back soon accompanied by Papa John.

Ruth looked so distressed. It hurt her so much to see her dear friend in such a tearful state. "Please God, give me the right words," she asked silently. "Marie, Ted did say that he saw John being taken away just before all the patriots came out of the woods to surprise them under the leadership of Colonel Morgan with his riflemen. He said they really know how to fight and he and Gilbert were lucky to get out of there alive. They saw a lot of their comrades killed on the battlefield. Their hearts are heavy as they dwell upon their experiences there. Ted and I are so thankful that they were not hurt." She walked over to Marie and put her arms around her. "Ted and I are so sorry about John but maybe he escaped. Let's not think the worse."

"I know, Ruth, that it is hard for you to be enthusiastic for a victory of the rebels as you call them but everything seemed to be looking up for us. We even have a flag of our own now. It was adopted in June you know. Then we have been losing battles right along until this last one at Saratoga. I shouldn't talk on like this because I know you don't agree with me but we have been friends so long. I remember back when we came over on the ship Anne and how we wanted our freedom. I just think, Ruth, that if we win this war against England you will enjoy freedom right along with us. You know it tells us in the Bible that there is a time for everything and I think that it is time we are on our own and not dependent on any country. I don't want to hurt you, Ruth. Just think about these things."

"Out friendship will not be hurt ever, Marie. I wouldn't want anything to happen to any of your sons. We just love them so much. Let's let God's will be done. We just love them so much. May God protect our sons and yours." With tears in her eyes Ruth prepared to go home. "I must leave now, Marie. I want to make a good dinner for the boys before they leave again tomorrow."

Marie walked her friend to the door and noticed Rachel on her way back with John. She hoped John had some answers. So many times she had gone through the same thing as Rachel was going through right now wondering if her husband was safe and then hearing all these rumors of how he was wounded or missing in action. She didn't know what she would have done if it hadn't been for her faith in God. She prayed for peace of mind for Rachel too as she looked to God for her help and her strength. She held the door open for Rachel and John as they came up the walk.

"I suppose you are in as much distress as Rachel is right now, Marie. Let's sit down here and talk this over," he said as he went over to his favorite chair. "In the first place we know our men surprised them soon after Ted saw the prisoners taken away. They couldn't have traveled very far before our victory. I surmise the prisoners escaped soon after the British guards heard the fighting going on.

John knows all the ways through the woods and would have no trouble coming home."

"Then why isn't he here, John?" Marie asked. "If Ted and Gilbert had time to get back home wouldn't he be able to make it back also?" she asked as she brushed the tears from her eyes. Rachel looked back and forth from one to the other and continued to softly sob.

"I don't really know but remember the time I was wounded in the French and Indian War. I was held up for weeks with a kind family along the way back home. They dressed my wounds and took care of me night and day. I will never forget them. Something like that could have happened to John. Let's not give up on him," he said as he walked over to Rachel and put his arm around her. "Just go home, Rachel, and we will all pray that we will see him soon. You need to be with Kathleen," and he led her out of the room and out of the door.

Day after day went by and still there was no news of John's whereabouts or of Daniel. Ted and Gilbert went back to serve with the British army. They all knew despite Ted's and Gilbert's dedication to the British they would do anything to seek their friends' escape back to Savannah.

John and Daniel had always enjoyed serving with Colonel Morgan/. He was a skilled rifleman and had taught his rangers the marksmanship and fighting skills that he used. John knew his sons were in the best place if they had to take part in this war. Daniel Morgan trained his riflemen well and the woods became a refuge and a place to plan their next move…a place to hide and communicate with their turkey calls. John knew that Daniel Morgan would not take lightly losing any of his men. If his son was taken prisoner Colonel Morgan would find a way to release him.

Marie was hardly sleeping nights as she was thinking and praying for John's release. Every day she thought she would soon hear from her sons. Her heart was hurting for Rachel. It was coming into November and they still had not heard from their sons. Marie was so sorry about John especially and they didn't know for sure about Daniel.

Rachel and Johanna came over daily to talk to Marie and pray with her for their husbands release if they were in prison on the English ships. Marie tried to keep their spirits up and show them all that God had delivered them from before they even came over to this new country. Marie knew that God had a plan for her sons.

It was a month later in the middle of the night that John and Marie were awakened by turkey calls. John quickly went to the door to be greeted by their two sons.

"Come in, come in," he said as he embraced them for the first time in months. "What has happened to you? We were so worried!" John kept talking on and on until Marie joined them. "What are you wearing?" she asked as she observed them in their tattered clothing. "We were waiting day after day. Johanna and Rachel were here every day with the girls. Oh, boys, I am so glad you are home. Tell us all about what happened to you." Marie felt lightheaded and quickly sat down before she would fall down.

"We will bring our wives over here and explain the whole thing to you. We are both so anxious to see them and our daughters. We have wanted to let you know that we are fine now. I guess you know that we won the war at Saratoga. We will be back in no time and then we can all get some rest," Daniel said as he went out the door with John limping beside him.

Marie and John hugged each other as they watched their sons leave to go to their homes. Marie hurried to make tea and brought out her bread she had made yesterday with some of her homemade jam. John kept watch of when they would all arrive back to their home. "We must be as quiet as possible, Marie. We never know who is listening and I know there are more people here loyal to the King than are with us. We don't have to worry about Ruth and Ted but there are plenty others who would think it their duty to stand by their King."

It wasn't long until they heard their sons coming with their wives and daughters. John quickly ushered them inside. Everyone was quiet as they lay the girls down on the floor wrapped in their quilts. They fussed a little but soon went back to sleep.

Everyone gathered around the table as John and Daniel told of their experiences. "I saw John taken prisoner," Daniel said. "There wasn't anything I could do about it at first. We were in the midst of a battle just as the prisoners were taken away by the British. We won that battle at Saratoga. I was there when General Burgoyne gave up his sword to General Gates. General Gates then returned the sword as a gesture of good will." Daniel's arm went around Johanna as she silently wept tears of happiness to be with her husband again. "John and I were serving under Colonel Dan Morgan. Colonel Morgan told me that we would not let John ever get to the prison ships. He had a plan to rescue him. The British were so sure of victory that they let down their guard and sent the prisoners away, using men that could have helped them fight, to be guards for their prisoners. As soon as victory was assured Colonel Morgan led our group through the woods to rescue John. We could see him from the woods. They had stopped for the night to camp out until the next morning. I was afraid John was hurt because he stayed in the one place all evening." Daniel looked exhausted as he pushed his blond hair away from his forehead. He looked as if he hadn't had a bath for weeks and he had let his beard grow for the more than a month since they had fled from the British army. "I found out John wasn't wounded as I first thought but he was bruised and his arm was broken from the treatment he received as the guards dragged him along the trail.

We made camp back in the woods so that John could mend. I set his arm as well as I could and washed his bruises and kept him quiet as he looked as if he also had a concussion. We only rescued John and another fellow. The whole group woke up before we could make our escape but we lost them in the woods. Colonel Morgan left us to go back to join the army.

Daniel looked like he could fall asleep any minute and John couldn't keep his eyes off Rachel. She was just as pretty as ever. Her strawberry blond hair hung down her back in beautiful waves. Coming from her bed, she hadn't taken time to dress or put up her hair.

Marie knew that it was time for everyone to go home and get some rest. "Let's talk over all this in the morning. We need to contact

George and Rebecca so that they can meet with us and hear from you both. How thankful I am that you are both back home safe. God is so good. "His mercy endureth forever." Marie went over and gave both of her sons kisses and hugs. She was so relieved that they were home safe. "John, I know you are weak yet but is your head feeling better? I can see your bruises are still there. They must have really beat you up."

"Mother, it is something I will try to forget. I didn't even know where I was for days on end. "You don't know how relieved I was when I woke up in the woods instead of on the British ship. I am so sleepy right now and I know Daniel is also."

Daniel and Johanna, John and Rachel quickly picked up their daughters and walked to their homes promising to come back at noon tomorrow to explain all that went on with their lives after John's capture.

Marie blew out the candle and with thankful hearts she and John went back to bed to get their much needed rest. "Oh, John, they both look like it has been a long time since they ate a good meal. And their clothes, we will have to get busy making some clothing for them. Thank God for Colonel Morgan. If our sons need to be in the army it is so nice that they are serving under a caring man."

"We will find out the whole story tomorrow, dear. Let's just get some sleep. It has been a trying two months. I'm just so glad that they are safe." They were both soon asleep, no longer bothered by their constant worry about their sons.

Everyone appeared at noon the next day. Rebecca, Johanna, Rachel and Mary brought dishes of food from home. The neighbors wouldn't think anything of the whole group coming for dinner. They were used to seeing the family all getting together. Rachel and Johanna came first with their daughters followed by George and Mary who had Daniel and John hid in their wagon. They went around to the back and were quickly ushered into the house. Marie told them all to sit down to the table and they would all eat before the boys told them their experiences. How happy they were to have them home safe. They knew the Tories would cause all kinds of trouble if they knew John and Daniel were home right now.

After everyone was finished with their meal they all sat around to listen to John and Daniel's experiences. "Well, I must say you both look better today than you did last night," Marie said as she gazed proudly at her two sons.

"I will start," Daniel said. "We still had clothes at home so we washed up and put clean clothes on for the first time in months. Of course, we tried to keep as clean as possible but it was hard living out in the forest…keeping away from the British soldiers. John didn't even know where he was for days. When he couldn't keep up with the horses on their way to the ships, they dragged the prisoners on the ground. I was wondering why John was so still when I observed him the evening we found where they were camping. He was out cold. I carried him away from there and God was with me. No one heard when we escaped. We heard a lot of noise after we came away from there so they must have discovered John missing after we left. We kept in contact with Colonel Morgan and his turkey calls. He couldn't stay with us as he had things to do in this war but he always left someone nearby to help us if we needed it. We were afraid to move John. I'm sorry but there was no way to contact any of you. I'll let John tell the rest."

All eyes turned to John. He still looked very weak. They knew Daniel had a hard time finding enough food. There was a brook nearby and Daniel was able to go into some field round about to get some vegetables. "I was so thankful that Daniel was there with me. He says I was out for a week and then I didn't know where I was. When the British soldiers heard the gunfire soon after we were on our way, they panicked and drove us unmercifully. We thought they would never stop beating us to keep everyone in line and moving. If anyone fell they just pulled them along sometimes hooking us to the wagons they had. I couldn't see or hardly breathe by the time they made camp. I don't remember Daniel even picking me up. I just know everyone was so exhausted that they had to stop and get some rest. They had us tied to the trees round about. I was so thankful I had a brother to care for me. I was constantly afraid I would be caught especially when Daniel would go to find food for us. I was so glad when Daniel thought it was safe to try to make it home. I missed all of you but especially Rachel and then Kathleen." Rachel held his hand as he talked. They had so much love for each other.

Marie dabbed her eyes with her handkerchief. Marie and John were so thankful that God had taken care of their son and sent him back home to them. "I hope you are staying home for awhile. We need to make you some clothing and you need to rest from your experiences."

"I could use you with the harvest you know but," and George stood up to talk to the whole family. "I imagine you just want to go back and finish what we started." He walked back and forth in front of them. "I would like to go myself but someone has to stay here at home. I realize Papa could not take care of everything on the plantation anymore and we need to raise crops that will benefit our military. We are proud of you, John and Daniel," and he gave each one of his brothers a hug.

Maxi wandered into the room and over to Marie who held him on her lap. The children all loved to play with him and moved a piece of yarn in front of her, making her jump off Marie's lap to chase it. The children were all laughing and coaxed her out of the room to play with them.

George did understand their wishes to be back in the fight. Their nation's freedom depended on them. "We are concerned about you both," he said as he pushed back his red hair from his forehead. "We will be praying for you. I know our armies aren't as well prepared as the British but I feel God is with us. It was so good that we had the Turtle, our first submarine. We really took care of the HMS Eagle when they bombed it. That was a 64 gun flagship and when the Turtle came under it with a bomb I imagine you could hear the sound for miles around. That was Admiral Howe's ship. I suppose he had a lot of explaining when the King heard about that. Oh, yes we will win this war. I know we will!"

"I agree," Daniel said," There is no way the British will win this war. They don't fight like we do. We know the territory and under Colonel Morgan we are able to get through the forest, climbing trees so that we can see what they are doing and as we hide in the brush their chances are slim to nothing to win this war for their

King. And what's more I don't think most of them care one way or another. They are anxious to just get it over with and get back with their families.

"We intend to go back with George tonight and tomorrow morning he will be able to take us to a safe place where we can join Colonel Morgan again," John said. Rachel looked up with sadness in her eyes. She was hoping John would be staying for awhile. "Are you well enough to go so soon, dear?" Kathleen was sitting in her Daddy's lap as he was talking.

Marie felt sad about this announcement too but she knew they all had to make sacrifices for their freedom and their children's freedom. No nation should have the power to rule them from across the sea. She knew what Rachel and Johanna were going through. So often she had waited for John to come back home especially during the French and Indian War. She knew John would be in the fight now but considering his age he was of more value helping George at the Plantation.

"These are hard times for our family," John said as he bid John and Daniel goodbye. "We will be praying for you. I know what it is to be a part of a conflict. I have confidence that we will win and you will be home soon but in the meantime you will have to be careful when you have a chance to come back home. The Tories are getting more powerful here all the time. Maybe your family can go with you out to the Plantation. Just stay hidden on the way out. No one would think anything of you bringing Johanna and Rachel with the baby girls out to the plantation for a few days. They have done that before and helped Mary with all her work in the house."

George went out the back way and prepared the wagon for his guests. John and Daniel followed George and quickly hid among his quilts in the front of the wagon bed. The horses were ready to start and pulled the wagon around to the front where the rest of their families climbed into the wagon. Mary sat with George in the front while he guided the horses away to the plantation.

Marie waved until they were out of sight. Rebecca stood by her side and both of them had tears in their eyes. They prayed that they would soon have victory and would be able to live a peaceful life here in Savannah.

Christmas was upon them before they realized it. Kathleen and Martha were growing so much and they were playing together just as Rachel and Johanna had hoped they would grow up to be friends and not just cousins. They were learning to share their dolls and teddy bears. Everyone in the family was so proud of them. There was just one thing that was missing in their lives. They didn't know the pleasure of a father's presence and love in their lives. There were so many men in the same situation. Marie decided not to have the special Christmas dinner she always had before. Everyone was gathering at the Plantation. If Daniel and John were able to make it back home they were sure it would be easier for them to meet at the plantation. Marie and John did the turkey and packing a few clothes to see them overnight, they left on Christmas Eve.

It was a cold winter night as they left their home in their carriage. Rachel and Johanna were bundled up in the back seat, Martha and Kathleen all wrapped up and cuddling in their mother's arms.

"Look at the stars, girls," Rachel said as they gazed up into the sky. "We must remember about the star that led the shepherds to Jesus." Johanna started singing "Silent Night" as Papa started the horses on their way. They really didn't know if they would see Daniel and John or not this Christmas but it was more likely they would try to make it to the plantation than that they would come to Savannah. There were so many Tories that could report them in Savannah. Martha fell asleep as they continued their journey. Kathleen was just about asleep but trying to sing along with them.

"When are Rebecca and Wesley coming?" Rachel asked Marie and John. The carriage hit a bit of ice in the road but slipped back on soon.

"They are coming tomorrow morning, Rachel. We thought if Daniel and John did come into town, which I don't think they would dare, that they would see Rebecca and Wesley and come out with them tomorrow," John said as he put down the reins. He knew the horses knew the way and needed no guidance from him. In his beautiful tenor voice he sang some Christmas songs to the girls.

Marie never tired of hearing him sing which brought back so many good memories of Christmas past.

Johanna was laughing. "I don't think the girls hear you, Papa. They seem to be sleeping. Don't stop singing though. I love to hear you sing. I always notice you singing as you work on all your projects. It thrills my heart."

John continued singing as they kept traveling to the plantation. It not only seemed to please his family but it took his mind off worrying about his sons. He knew how tragic war could be on the men not only physically but mentally and emotionally as well. He didn't know if his sons were living yet or sick. Word had spread that the soldiers were suffering from all kinds of illness. They were not getting the right food to stay healthy. Some were even coming down with Smallpox. John knew that George Washington had many vaccinated against Smallpox and he knew his sons had that done just before the last time they came home. George Washington had Smallpox years before and didn't want any of his men to get the disease. He hoped Daniel and John would find their way to the plantation and celebrate Christmas with the family. Yes, singing had always been a way for him to keep his sanity even during the prison time. He had continued singing since he left Ireland. Marie loved to hear him sing. Just as he was singing, "Silent Night" again they entered the lane leading up to the plantation house.

Mary was waiting for them at the door when they arrived. She greeted them all with hugs and kisses. Marie really appreciated Mary as her daughter in-law. God had so blessed their family. Daniel and John had to be safe. They were under god's care.

"Come in quickly," Mary said. "George is waiting for you in the barn. Our prayers have already been answered. George is with his brothers now. They came home through the swamplands. Colonel Morgan told them they could all go home because the British were not fighting at this time. You will hear the whole story from them. We are just so excited."

Everyone came into the house. "I guess we better not go out to the barn all at once. You never know who is watching. Ruth and Ted knew we were coming here but I know they wouldn't tell anyone," Marie said as they discussed the best way to handle this surprise.

"I'll go out and take the horses to the barn," John said. "If they came through the swamplands, I imagine they are in a bad state. Do you have any clothes to fit them in here, Mary?"

Mary went to their bedroom and picked out two outfits of George's she thought would fit them. "Maybe if they come in one at a time, anyone passing by would think it was George."

Johanna and Rachel could hardly wait to see their husbands. This was going to be a wonderful Christmas in spite of the war. John went out to put the horses in the barn and to bring the outfits to his sons. Daniel was first to come into the house. Johanna ran to him as soon as he entered the door. There was crying and laughing all together as she hugged her husband. He looked as if he hadn't eaten for awhile and there were scratches on him from all the branches of the bushes and trees they had gone past as they went through the swamp. "We kept our muskets dry though." Daniel said. "It was a cold walk but we kept going so we could get home to our families. It wasn't just John and me. There were about forty of us going through but we made it. The British are busy with their parties and celebrations for Christmas." Daniel picked up Martha. She was so warm and cuddly. She was hugging her Papa. You could see she was so glad he was home again.

Marie was getting some food ready for her sons. No one else was hungry as they ate before they came. John came in and received the same reception as Daniel did. It was just a few minutes before George came in with Papa and they were all talking at once. Anne, Marian, Virginia and Joshua came down the stairs when they heard all the commotion. It was late and they all needed to go to bed.

"We didn't want to disturb the whole family," Daniel said. "We just wanted to be here with you on Christmas. We sent letters but I suppose you didn't get half of them. It was so cold coming through some parts of the swamp. The water was almost up to our waist and we had all we could do to keep our muskets out of the water. There were about twenty of us all together but when we came up to Savannah we all separated and went to our various homes."

John turned away from Rachel and Kathleen to speak to them all. "We were so anxious to get home. I think we are winning this war but it is taking a lot out of us. I have never been so hungry and cold. I know you sent us away with plenty of blankets and clothing but we couldn't keep everything for ourselves. We had to share with the other men. I am sure their families sent them off with food and clothing too but sometimes when we are called upon to defend ourselves or to go into battle against them we have to leave our possessions behind. The officers suffer right along with us. George Washington is sleeping in a tent along with his men until the cabins are all built. The officers are very good to us."

Marie was so touched by the hardships her sons had to endure. "I will fix you something to eat right now. You both have lost a lot of weight and I imagine this is one of the days you haven't been any place to eat."

"We have brought food also, Mother. Let's have a Christmas Eve supper just as we always had in the past," Rachel said as she hurried to help Marie get out the food and set the table. Mary lit all the candles on the Christmas tree. "We didn't think we would have much of a celebration because you would not be here," Marie said as she looked lovingly at her sons. This was going to be a good Christmas of 1777 and she was looking forward to 1778 when certainly there would be victory and they would be a free nation.

Chapter 11

Marie walked to the church today. John wasn't feeling well so he stayed behind. The weather was refreshing on this spring day. Each yard passed by was beautiful with all the spring flowers sprouting up. The smell of peach blossoms filled the air. It made her feel a little better to see nature in all its glory. Marie's dress fell in lovely folds switching along the cobblestone walk. She was wearing John's favorite dress of sky blue. She was concerned about him. She wasn't sure if he was just worried about their sons in the war or if he had taken a chill working out at the plantation helping George. They had not heard from Daniel nor John for this past five months. They knew how the prisoners were treated on the prison ships. Captives lived on bilge-tainted meat and wormy biscuit. She heard disease was rampant on the prisoner ships. She prayed to God her sons were not on any of those ships.

Lost in her thoughts, Marie was startled to hear her name called as she approached the church. "Marie, Marie!," Ruth said, catching her breath. "I was trying to catch up with you but you didn't hear me. I see you are walking also. Ted didn't feel up to coming today. How is John? I didn't see him at all yesterday," They paused as a carriage was coming down the cobblestone road they needed to cross. They proceeded to cross after the carriage passed.

"John hasn't been feeling very well this past week. I don't know if he worked too hard helping George or if he is coming down with something. I just hope Daniel and John are well. You hear of all kinds of ailments in the military. I suppose it is the same with the British army."

"I don't worry about our sons. It seems they get enough to eat and all winter long they stayed in the cities near where they were based. Our Generals take care of our men so we are not worried about our sons except in the fighting of course."

"Yes, we hear about the British Army and how they are not a threat to anyone during the winter months. I know there is danger out there however. Someday we will have our own country but let's not fuss about the war when we plan to sit in church and hear the sermon. John and I still count you as our friends despite your views on this war. That is a beautiful dress, Ruth. Did you make it yourself?"

Ruth, pleased at the compliment, paused after crossing the street, "This dress is made of the material our sons brought from Philadelphia. I made it up. I still sew some even at my age." Marie had given up sewing. Her rheumatism just wouldn't let her handle a needle or even take one stitch. She didn't know how she was going to proceed with helping at their quilting meetings.

"Just keep sewing as long as you can, Ruth," Marie commented. "I have given up sewing entirely. I feel at a loss when we all get together to quilt and to knit socks. I try to help in other ways…. serving the refreshments and anything else that needs taking care of. It is terrible to not be able to do the things I could do when I was younger."

Ruth felt so sorry for her friend. "We appreciate all the things you do for us…why, just opening your house up for our meetings is help enough. Your daughter and daughters-in law make up for you with all the stitching they do. Well, here we are. I think we must be a little late. Our Pastor is usually out here greeting people."

The first hymn was already being sung as they took their places in the pew. As Marie looked around she realized she was seeing more Loyalists than Patriots in the congregation. Of course, you didn't know where everyone stood on this war. Some of her friends had made a decision to not let anyone know where their sympathies lay.

Marie and Ruth joined in with the singing. Marie settled back to hear the sermon. She liked Rev. Roberts sermons despite his youth. He seemed led by God. John and she prayed for him every day. She didn't know whether he was a Loyalist or not. He never brought the war into his sermons except to tell the congregation of his grief for all the injuries and deaths on both sides of the war. Marie glanced to the right and saw her daughters-in-law there with their baby daughters. They were walking now and getting into everything. It must be hard for them to keep the girls in their pew. Her prayer was that they would grow up to come to know Jesus as their Savior and to be safe in this war.

The service was over soon and Marie felt better for being a part of this meeting. She knew it would do John a lot of good to come also. He worried so much about their sons. Her granddaughters escaped from their mothers and ran to her almost before she entered the aisle. All the church members greeted each other commenting on what a beautiful day it was. Even Marie's aches and pains didn't bother her as much today.

"Grandma, Grandma," Kathleen said, "We good today. Did you see?"

"Yes, honey, I noticed you sitting so still up there with your Mama. You and Martha were both good little girls. I suppose you will have a treat now when you get home. Martha and Kathleen giggled and nodded yes. Marie bent down and picked up Martha, giving her a hug. Ruth picked up Kathleen. Ruth was so glad Marie and John shared times they had with these precious grandchildren. "Are you going to give Auntie Ruth a hug, Kathleen?" Marie asked as she gave Martha another hug. A few of the older ladies gathered around to see these sweet little girls. Johanna and Rachel finished visiting with their friends and, picking up their little girls, were on their way. Sometimes they all met for dinner at Marie and John's home but decided to go home and let John have some rest. Rebecca and Wesley were not in church this morning either. Marie decided to call on her in the afternoon.

Ruth and Marie walked out of the door soon after the girls left. Rev. Roberts greeted them and asked after John's and Ted's health.

He indicated he knew these were trying days…every day full of worry about the men fighting this war….days when everyone was looking for a solution to end the war.

Ruth and Marie started home refusing any offers of rides to take them home. It wasn't far and would do them good despite their battle with rheumatism. "Ruth, I think the walk will do us good but I know I will be aching when I get home. With a little rest it will not take long to recover. It is a beautiful day for a walk like this. Remember how we would walk with our children? It brings memories back when I see my grandchildren growing up."

"It does for me too, Marie. Just look at all the beautiful flowers coming up this Spring in all the squares. I never forgot how wise Colonel Oglethorpe was when he designed all these squares. I imagine they will be here for generations. I sometimes wish we had not sent our sons over to England for their education. They only had their summers here and we missed all the growing up you experienced with your children. Then again they wouldn't have learned as much here. They have good positions in the British Army."

"Yes, but I think our sons would be closer if you had not sent them off to England. Anyway, Ruth, what did England ever do for us? We were put in jail for our debts and however could we pay anything back if we were in jail? she asked.

"I remembered growing up in England and I wanted our sons to have the same experience. I understand how you feel about it. I don't know what we would do if the Patriots win this war. We are considering just going to Canada if that happens. There are a lot of Loyalists that have done that already. We would have a lot of friends there but then we would miss you too so I don't know how this will all turn out. Only God knows."

"How we would miss you and Ted, Ruth. You are like part of our family. We had so many experiences together. Let's hope for the best and leave it in God's hands." Marie continued on their walk with Ruth, saddened by their conversation but they were almost home and they parted as friends.

As Marie opened the door she noticed how quiet the house seemed. She thought that John would have felt better and at least set the table for their meal. She walked into their bedroom and found him still in bed. She approached the bed and touching his forehead she found him in a fever. "Oh, John, I see you are worse than when I left this morning."

"I am sure not feeling well…aching all over. I guess I have the flu. Better stay away from me until I feel better," he said in his hoarse voice.

"I'll make you tea and I have some soup I can warm up, dear. I'm so sorry you are ill. I wonder where you caught the flu. Was George feeling well when you left? Do you want me to fetch the Doctor?"

John turned over in bed. "George was fine, Marie. I just need to rest and I could drink some tea. I don't know where I could have caught this but I am sure with a little rest I will be over it soon. I don't need the Doctor."

Marie hurried out of the room to make the tea and soup. She wondered about Ted. She hoped this wasn't something that would go around their community. She hoped her sons did not get this kind of flu. So many of the military died of diseases and not just fighting in the war. Marie proceeded to boil some onions to steam near John's bed. She had some Sarsaparilla roots to make the tea for John. She knew he would complain about all these preparations but she was confident it would help him overcome the flu along with her prayers. She carried the steaming onion mixture into the bedroom to find John still hot with his fever. At least he was awake and could breathe in some of this onion mixture.

"I knew you would start all this, Marie. I think just the rest would help me get over this flu and not all these other things," he groaned.

Marie couldn't help but tease John. He didn't know how to be sick. He had enjoyed good health all his life. "I guess I will have to go for the Doctor, Dear, and then he will use some extreme treatment like blood letting. Do you want that?" she asked.

John sat up on the side of the bed. "I think we will try the onions and the tea and if I get the rest for a few days I will be feeling better. Marie, stay away from me and tell our family to stay away until I get better, and please don't get the Doctor. I think he has done more harm than good." He went into a coughing spell but soon was drinking his tea.

Marie continued to care for John and prayed for him to get well. He was a strong man and with Marie's care was soon up and sitting with her at the table eating regular food. They heard that the flu was taking a toll on their military also, in fact taking more lives than the military who had come under enemy fire. Ted had contracted the flu also but was soon well with Ruth's care. Marie looked for it to make them sick also but they were thankful that it didn't effect them.

On March 16 everyone was excited because King George had sent a Peace Commission to Philadelphia to meet all America's demands. Ruth and Ted were thrilled. Finally everything would be peaceful again. They came over to rejoice with John and Marie.

"My, you both are looking happy. I suppose you have heard from your sons," Marie said as she opened the door to greet Ted and Ruth.

Marie and John came in and sat down with them at the table. "We were just finishing our lunch. Did you eat already? I just made a chicken pie and it certainly too much for us."

"No, no, Marie," Ruth replied. "We just finished our lunch. We would have a cup of tea with you if you have it. We came over to tell you the good news. One of the English soldiers stopped at our house to tell us the news of this Peace Commission. We don't know anymore than what he told us as our sons haven't contacted us about it."

Marie put two cups on the table and poured them each a cup of tea. "Are they giving us our demands then so we can live as a free nation?"

"Well," Ted said, "They said they would give us all our demands except freedom. We would still be part of the British Empire. Sounds good to us."

John was furious but didn't want to show anything but love to these dear neighbors. They had gone through so much together. "I hope and pray the congress does not accept this kind of agreement. That is what this whole war is about. To gain our freedom. We would be defeated if we accepted anything like what you were saying. Don't you understand, Ted? We will not be ruled by a country overseas. We will not lose this war and that is what this whole treaty is about. We would be the losers and our children would live under English rule. We will not let that happen."

"Calm down, John," Ted replied. "We don't want this to come between us. We have confidence in our King. He will not mistreat us but wants to join us in making this a strong nation and I know they will help us anyway they can."

Ruth and Marie looked at each other afraid their friendship would not hold up through these trials. "Let's just hope for peace," Marie said. "I know God will see us though this with His will to be done."

Ruth and Marie turned the conversation away from the war and soon they were all talking like old friends. Congress did not accept the King's peace treaty and the war continued.

The summer went well and John was able to help George with the crops. Marie was already making plans for their Christmas celebration. She was sure their sons would come home from the war and that there would be a peaceful solution by that time. She knew the majority of the people living in Savannah were Loyalists but she also knew that their Patriot army was getting experience and as a result was successful in a lot of the battles. They had 60 Patriot militia just outside of Savannah ready to protect them if the British try to take over. In June, John and Marie put up their new flag to hang in their living room. The flag was a year old now. They were afraid to hang it outdoors because it might cause trouble with the Loyalists there. More of them were moving into the community all the time and hanging out their Union Jacks. Ted and Ruth continued to welcome British soldiers into their home. They said they were carrying out the King's Quartering Act. Ruth continued to make them meals when they were in their home. Marie knew that was too much for Ruth. She was even older than Marie and had aches and pains the same as any older person.

October came and there was still no word from their sons. John continued to help George in the fields. Marie was truly worried about their sons. The boats that came in sometimes carried mail and she thought for sure they would get some letters soon. She prayed continually that someone would come into Savannah that had seen John and Daniel. Marie hoped at least they would be home for Christmas. She felt so sorry for Rachel and Johanna. Marie understood how your life was when your husband was fighting in the war. She was so glad that John was through with that now and they could spend so much time together. Sometimes she rode out to the plantation with her husband to help Mary put up vegetables or in the spring with her cleaning. She always enjoyed her times with Mary. Marie had started making her Christmas gifts in June. She felt she had to have more time to get them done in her older years. She seemed to be able to make baskets yet but any sewing was out of the question.

It was noontime in November when George came in to see his parents. He was riding his horse that was unusual for him so Marie and John knew something had happened at home. He quickly tied his horse at the rail in the front and ran in to tell his parents the news. He was all out of breath.

"Let me sit down, Mother," he said as he sat at the kitchen table. "I was just talking to Daniel. John is doing well now. He stayed back with Colonel Morgan and his troops. Daniel didn't dare come into town or stay very long with us. He wanted us all to know that they are fine but the British are focusing on the South right now urging the Loyalists to join them in fighting for England. Daniel didn't even dare to come into the house. When I went out to do the chores I heard this turkey call coming from the barn and I found Daniel in there. He wants us all to be careful because he thinks they might be heading for Savannah. Of course, they have a lot of territory to go through in order to get to Savannah. Please notify Rachel and Johanna. I must go back immediately."

John and Marie hugged George and sent him on his way. This was a sad day for Marie and John. They felt so helpless but knew there was nothing they could do to help their sons. Let's walk to Rachel and Johanna's," Marie said. "Then we will stop by Rebecca's to give her the news. I wonder about Charles and Alice also," Marie said as she brought a sweater to John and picked up one for herself also. "It is getting cool out, dear, especially this early in the morning."

"I wouldn't worry about Charles and Alice, Marie. I imagine the British will treat the citizens on the Island well. They will need them to help enter Savannah. Of course, I don't know if they will come by sea or through the swamplands. Anyway, let's hope our men will be able to defend our city."

It wasn't far to their daughter's in-law's homes. Rachel burst into tears when they told her but Johanna kept calm as usual. Johanna was very concerned about Daniel coming in secret to the plantation. "I have made new clothes for him too. I so wish that he could have come here. I'm in constant worry about his health and how he fares with the colder weather. How did he look Papa?"

"George said he looked fine, Rachel. He just couldn't take a chance to be seen with all the Loyalists around here. I'm sure he is well on his way to join the rest of the Rangers. Don't worry. Let's put this in God's hands. Shall we walk over to Rebecca's? She and Wesley should know about this also."

Rachel and Johanna got the girls up and they were soon on their way to Rebecca's. She knew immediately that something was wrong when she saw so many of her family members on her doorstep this early in the morning. She knew it must be sad news, looking at Rachel's face streaked with tears. John was carrying Kathleen who was rubbing her eyes as it was early for her to be up and about.

"Come in, all of you," Rebecca said. "It must be bad news you are carrying. Sit down and I will make you all a cup of tea. Aunt Ruth brought some over yesterday. She also gave me a loaf of her delicious bread. I'll get out the jam and we will sit and talk around the table."

"It is terrible news," Marie said as she sat down at the table and took out her handkerchief and wiped her eyes. "I just don't know what we will do. The British are getting closer to Savannah."

"I thought we had an army out there to protect us," Rachel said. "We have never been afraid before, Mother."

"I heard that there are just 1,550 troops to guard our city. They will never be able to hold it. There are too many British troops to fight against our men," Papa said. "I know Ted and Ruth will stand by us and do all they can to help us."

Johanna listened to everything Papa was saying and it terrified her. They couldn't all be under the umbrella of safety with Ruth and Ted. She bowed her head in a moment of silent prayer. "I have a sister in Spanish Florida. She lives right across the border of Florida. I wonder if Martha and I would be able to escape to my sister. Daniel would want me to seek safety for our daughter. Wesley, what do you think our chances would be?"

"I suppose it would work. I wonder if you should wait until we see if Savannah can be defended. We have citizens here that would join in the fight to keep our city free. Let's not give up so easily. Anyway we should all be safe…The British military would still need a lot of our services and would depend on us to provide them with food and clothing. I don't see them making everyone prisoners. They would probably need shoes from the cobbler, a blacksmith they always need, then lodging and a lot of other needs if they plan to occupy this city. Let's hope it never happens and if it does, Johanna, we can all work together to get you out of the city."

"I'll leave it to your judgment, Papa. I don't want to stay here and Daniel will never see us. It has been so long since we were together. We must pray that we will soon have peace with England and we will have a free country."

They were all in agreement that they would wait and see how their military fared to protect the city. It was in God's hands. Maybe God would work through the Liberty Boys who met at Peter Tondie's tavern weekly. The tavern had recently opened and was in competition to Peggy and Frank's boarding house.

There continued to be rumors of war all through November and even up to Christmas. Marie and John decided they would do the best they could with Christmas. John went out to cut down a tree for Christmas and Marie decorated it with popcorn and different ornaments the children had made. Marie put all the presents she made under the Christmas tree. George and Mary came with Anne, Marian, Virginia and Joshua. They came before dawn on Christmas day avoiding coming in contact with any Red Coats.

They ate breakfast with Marie and John. It wasn't long until Wesley and Rebecca came with Pricella, James, David and Emily. Johanna and Rachel came in with their beautiful little daughters. They didn't ask any of their friends. They knew their friends would all prefer to stay at home and the threat of war was over for them. As soon as it was dark George and Mary along with their children left for home. They didn't know if they were safer staying out at the plantation or if it would be safer in Savannah. Time would tell. Everyone slept well that night in their own homes. They could feel God's protection for them.

The 26th of December through the 28th of December seemed to be ordinary days until the evening of the 28th when they heard the echo of war surrounding them. The Liberty Boys had left soon after dark to guard the city and the military was surrounding the city. The residents had no idea if the patriots could hold their city or not. Toward midnight the firing stopped and everything was quiet. There was still no word of who was the victor in this fight. Marie and John kept praying and when the noise of battle stopped they decided to get some rest and wait until morning. At dawn the fighting resumed and as the sun came up over the city the noise of the troops continued. The gate of the city was forced open and the Red Coats entered in perfect formation. The British were victorious and the Loyalists were out welcoming them into their city. Marie and John noticed Ted and Ruth had joined them. They wondered if Ted and Ruth would see their sons today as their comrades marched through the city and around all the squares.

Chapter 12

Everything looked bleak for John and Marie this morning of January 1, 1779. They were so disappointed their army could not stop the British from occupying their city of Savannah. They were saddened by the loss of the Patriots' lives but still held on to the belief that freedom was worth the sacrifices of their people. They could see the British Military going up and down their streets as they kept order among the citizens. "I wonder, John, if we will ever have freedom in our lifetime. I keep wondering how our sons fared in all this and we didn't even hear from George and Mary."

"We have to trust our military more than that, dear. I am sure they have a plan to rescue us. It isn't like them to forget about defending us. Let's have breakfast now and we will see how the day goes. I know the British soldiers will not bother us unless we do something to raise their suspicions. We need to visit Ruth and Ted so that they will associate us with them.

Marie sighed as she lay out the breakfast for them. She hoped John was right and they soon would have their city back. Their founder would be distraught if he could see the situation their city was in now. Rebecca walked in just as they were finishing their breakfast and their devotions. Rebecca was the picture of her mother when Marie was in her 40's with her black hair and almost 5 ft. 5 inches height. John could see that she was disturbed and walked over to hug her. "What is wrong, Becky? Did someone try to stop you from coming here?"

"No, no, Papa, nothing like that. In fact the soldiers seem just intent on doing their job without any of us interfering. No, I heard that James Wright has been sent back to be our governor. You know how much we suffered under his rule. Especially, George had to buy all those stamps that had been imposed on them since the stamp act. He rules with an iron hand!"

"Sit down, Becky, and have a cup of tea with us. It might be a lot different this time. I look for our army to try to retake our city and he will soon be without a job here. Hopefully the King will bring him back home again." Becky kissed her mother on the cheek and sat down beside her. She hoped Mother and Papa would remain safe here.

"I know Peggy will be safe. As long as she has rooms in her boarding house everything will be fine. She can house a lot of the soldiers there." Becky had continued to help at times with all the washing that Peggy had to do for the tenants. Becky picked up one of the scones her mother had made this morning. She always felt better after visiting her parents. Marie poured a cup of tea for Becky and refilled John's cup.

Becky stirred her tea and looked up with tears in her eyes. "You know, we lost 83 soldiers in that fight which took over our city. What grieves me is that we don't know what happened to the 453 prisoners they took. Did they put them on their prisoner ships? Did they half kill them getting the prisoners to the ships as they almost killed Daniel? We don't even know if George and Mary survived.

Dear Lord, we don't know how anyone in our family fared." Becky put down her head and wept. "Now, James Wright has come back into the picture and I know he shows no mercy. He just cheated some of our Indian friends and now he owns eleven plantations and more than 500 slaves. Mother….Papa…What are we going to do?"

Marie left her seat at the table to comfort her daughter. She felt the same way. She couldn't see a light at the end of the tunnel. Yet, she knew that God understood their need and somehow, someway, He would solve their problem. He didn't bring them here to Georgia from prison to have them in another prison. God had a plan. Tears blurring her eyes she hugged Becky. "Let's just leave all this with God, honey. We do not see the future but it is in God's hands." Becky stayed a little while but then headed back to her family.

Papa walked her to the door. "Now, Becky don't do anything to disturb the soldiers. If one approaches you on the cobblestone walk step off and let him proceed. We don't know yet how well they will behave to the citizens of Savannah. Be careful now," Papa stepped outside with her in this frigid weather of January. Becky hurried home determined to avoid any of the Red Coats at all cost. She didn't know what this world was coming to that you could be held prisoner in your own city. She just wished she had stayed in the country but of course you had no way of telling what course the British Army would take to keep all residents in their place. She hoped George and Mary were safe.

It was the summer of 1779 and they still had no news from George. John decided he had to know how George and Mary and family fared. He was counting on his age to get him through the gates of the city. He thought even with the occupation of the city there had been no problems with the citizens for the British Military and if he told them he was in the habit of helping George with the crops that they would not deny him passage to the country. Marie was afraid for his safety but she felt the same urge to try to see if George and Mary were safe. Ted and Ruth continued to help them whenever they could but they had discovered no news of the plantations outside of their gates. Ted continued to back the English government and thought this was all nonsense to try to pull away from their home country. He did not want any harm to come to his friends however. Ruth continued to hide her true feelings from everyone but Marie. "I hope John will be safe, Marie. Anything we can do please tell us. When John is ready to go let's gather together to pray for his safety," she said as she walked to the door and out into the beautiful summer day. Marie agreed and went to the Carriage house to tell John they were meeting with him for prayer before he went.

John brought his two work horses around to the carriage house. He hitched them up to his small wagon which he always took out to the plantation in this season to take home the produce John gave him for his own use and to sell to the market. He had put a little hay in the bottom of the wagon. He was soon ready and Marie went over to the Miller home to give them the news of John's departure. Marie had just served one of the British guests his breakfast and told him they were going next door for prayer. The soldier knew they did that quite often so thought nothing about it. They quickly walked over and met with their friends in the carriage house. The horses had been isolated for so long they were past ready to start on this journey. "John, you know you are taking a risk but we don't blame you for trying," Ted said. "I want you to know that I am still a loyal English Citizen living here in Savannah. We aren't all against you Patriots, John. Even in England there are some Tories and some are Whigs. The King's party of Tories are in the majority right now but there are even Lords that are debating in the House of Lords that they should let the colonies have their freedom. Even some of the Military they sent here are not for this war with us. They are working for the Crown and are anxious to get it over with so they can go home again. Let's join hands as we pray."

Ted had never expressed his views of the war this way before. His friends had never discussed the way they felt with him as they didn't know his views were not so different from their views. He still stood for England and wanted everything to go back to the way it was before. Ted seldom led them in prayer but this was a special time and he was concerned for John's safety. As they all joined hands and bowed their heads, Ted led them in prayer. "Almighty God, Father of all mercies, we thine unworthy servants do give thee most humble and hearty thanks for all Thy goodness and loving-kindness to us and to all men. We thank thee for our creation, preservation and all the blessings of this life; but above all, for thine inestimable love in the redemption of the world by our Lord Jesus Christ. We pray you will keep John safe as he goes out to the countryside. May he find George and his family safe. We pray for our sons, Ted and Gilbert as British soldiers and we pray for John and Marie's sons, John and

Daniel. May they never meet each other in this war for harm but may they always keep their friendship with each other regardless of what side they are on. Thank you for keeping them safe so far in this war. May your will be done in this conflict and may we have peace in these colonies again. Through Jesus Christ, our Lord, to whom with thee and the Holy Ghost be all honour and glory, world without end. Amen.

The horses by now were getting more anxious to get going and as they released each others hand, John quickly bid them all goodbye and thanked Ted for his prayer. John climbed up on the wagon seat and gave his horses their signal to go.

"May God keep John safe," Marie murmured as John turned the corner and continued to the outside gate. Ruth gave Marie a hug and said, we need to get back home, dear. Remember the hymn we sang in England before all these troubles came upon us. I forget the name of it but the first verse went like this, "My times are in thy hand: My God, I wish them there; My life, my friends, my soul, I leave entirely to thy care." So let's do that and some day I know this war will be over."

Ted and Ruth returned home where a few British soldiers sat at their table. They all seemed so young to Ted and Ruth and so far away from their homes. They tried to make them feel at home not because they were British but because they were young men like their sons and they needed a place to feel at home. The soldiers were very respectful to the couple and did not cause them any trouble.

John had no trouble getting out of the gates and on his way to the plantation. The guards asked if there was any produce to take home to remember them. John surmised that George had to give all his produce to the British military and probably everyone there that were true to the Crown. He was there in no time and George was out in the barn taking care of the horses. He looked up in surprise to see Papa come in with the wagon. He ran to the wagon to welcome him. "We keep wondering about you and Mother," George said as he greeted his father.

John climbed down from the wagon. "We have been wondering about you too. I imagined all the plantations would be burned to the ground because we hear what terrible things are happening in other places."

"They didn't seem to bother us, Papa. I think they are leaving us alone and plan on confiscating our crops. I hear rumors that our armies are getting ready to take back Savannah. I don't think the British Military will stand for that. I think they will try to wipe us out if they win the battle again. Let's go in the house. Mary has been studying with Joshua today. The girls have been helping put up blackberry jam. Mary will want to give you some to take back home."

As they approached the back door the grandchildren ran out to greet their grandfather. Mary was right behind them. Maxi was running after them and came up to John rubbing himself against his legs and purring as he picked him up. John was overcome with all the attention. He praised God for his family's safety in these perilous times. There were hugs and kisses all around. A group of British Infantry proceeded down the road as John followed the family into their home. John took for granted that his every step would be watched so he took care to not cause any problem.

"Sit down, Papa, sit down. Have a cup of tea. Mary has made scones too so let's gather around the table and hear the latest news of Savannah. John was overjoyed these family members were safe. He thanked God for keeping them safe in all this wartime they were enduring. "Everything seems fine there as long as we don't cause any trouble. They claimed their right to Quarters wherever the commanding officer chose to put them but they didn't try to set the city on fire so you can imagine how thankful we are for that. You haven't heard anything from John or Daniel, have you? I thought they might contact you before they would try to enter Savannah." John sighed as he drank some more tea. George thought Papa's hair looked even whiter than the last time he saw him. The young people knew their family was in trouble and were quiet during the conversation.

George looked so much like Papa and was a picture of him at a younger age with his very red hair and his air of authority. "None of the military has stopped here for a long time. I guess the last time was when they first took over Savannah. I think they are just waiting for the crops to grow and then I look for them to confiscate all that we have. I hope they will leave a little bit for our family including our family living in Savannah. You can take back some of this blackberry jam. If you give a little to the Guards at Savannah they might be more interested in letting you come out here."

"I don't know, George," Papa said as he bowed his head," what we can do but take one day at a time and try to live with them as best we can. Of course we need to keep in constant prayer. Maybe our army will come in and rescue us. I guess John and Daniel would try to come here before they would try to tackle the British Military in Savannah. So far there has been no sign of them."

Mary knew Papa would want to get back home as soon as possible so she looked up a basket that would fit a couple dozen jars of Blackberry jam to take back home to Mother. She knew they would share it with the rest of the family in Savannah. She hoped he wouldn't be stopped and the jam confiscated for the British guards there. Anne put in some scones she had made and Marian put in the cookies she had made yesterday. They missed having their Grandma there but they knew these were hard times. In fact, it seems like most of their life was filled with fear and uncertainty. If it wasn't for their faith in God, Anne did not know what would become of them. Everyone was afraid to travel so they were more or less isolated and rarely saw any friends. Anne missed seeing her girlfriend, Greta and Greta's brother, Andy (well, especially Andy). She supposed he was getting more involved in the Sons of Liberty and maybe off to this war. Marian was always happy if she was reading or doing some needlework. Virginia was happy when her grandfather came to see them. She missed all her relatives who lived in Savannah. Joshua was waiting to get old enough to join the Sons of Liberty.

John agreed with George and knew it was time to head back home. He doubted if Marie would even taste the jam he brought back. He knew it would be taken from him.

If they only knew as they were talking of the terrible times for them that even now this May of 1779 that the American government ordered General McIntosh back to Georgia to assist Lincoln to put together a plan to take over Savannah. French Admiral D'estaing was sailing in the French West Indies and would be there to help them attack Savannah. The French had helped so much in recent years to win their freedom from the British.

John arrived home safely with one jar of the jam. The guards had taken the rest of the jars and laughingly told him they were looking forward to the produce in the future.

It was September before D'estaing was able to put in at the mouth of the Savannah River with his 20 ships and 11 frigates. He immediately sent a demand for Prevost, the British General in charge of British Savannah to surrender immediately. Instead Prevost strengthened the enforcements around the city.

All through September, Marie and John knew something was going on. They knew about the ships off their shores but they didn't know where their sons were serving at this time. Marie was hoping the ships were here to liberate their city. She knew they had to still be careful, constantly listening for news of the American military. It gave them hope to hear the Wasp was anchored right near Savannah.

They heard a lot of good things about this ship. It looked like the liberation would take place soon. They took care not to disagree with any of the British troops or get in their way. John could not leave the city anymore. It was too dangerous. Marie wanted to get out their new flag and be ready to wave it when their soldiers came marching in victory over the British but John said they should wait until they see who would be victorious. They could hear sounds of battle everywhere especially near the river and the swampland. ON October 9, 1779 Lincoln and D'estaing launched a heavy artillery bombardment while French and American infantry attacked the city. Polish Count Casimir Pulaski fought with the American side and was shot and killed by the British army. When the fighting was over the Tories were rejoicing and the Americans were stunned. They would still be under British rule. Eight hundred French and American soldiers lay dead. It was a sad day for all of them. Marie, with tears running down her face, put their flag back in its secret place. This must be the Lord's will for them at this time. She had no doubt that the day would come when the American flag would fly over their city of Savannah. Her faith in God would get her through these days until she saw this happen.

When the British had the city under control again the daily activities of the citizens proceeded as before. Marie and John wanted all the children to gather together for prayer and discussion of how they should proceed with their life here in this British controlled city. George needed to see how his parents fared and decided to try to get past the guards to visit his family. He knew the guards looked forward to all the produce he provided for them and their horses and also that he was friends with Ruth and Ted. The guards knew George as well as John so they ushered the whole family into the city.

It was early morning when there was a knock at the door. Marie went to the door. Johanna stood there with Martha in her arms. She was looking fearfully over her shoulder. "Come in quickly, dear," Marie said as she brought them into the house, hugging Johanna and Martha as they came in. "I hope you were careful but we noticed the military don't seem to be stopping the citizens as yet. Do you know if Rachel and Kathleen will be here?"

"It is terrifying to be out on the streets but we wanted to come, Mother." Johanna put Martha down. She didn't usually carry her around anymore. She was getting heavy and wanted to walk or run anyplace she went. "Rachel and Kathleen should be here soon and Becky said she would be over soon. Wesley is home and will come with her and the family. Oh, this is so terrible. I thought we would be free again but instead we are under the same rule as before."

Ruth and Ted came in next. Ruth hugged Marie and neither could speak for the tears coming down their faces. "Oh, Marie we came with sadness in our hearts. We lost Gilbert. Just right outside the city." She sobbed as Marie led her over to a chair to sit down. "He was part of the reinforcements General Prevost sent in. He was fighting alongside his friend, Ted, and Ted carried him outside the gates of the city. He died instantly. Help us, dear ones, to have a funeral service for him. We loved him so much. It's not right, Marie that your son would go before the parents," and she continued to cry. John and Marie had their arms around their friends trying to comfort them as best they could. "We will do anything you want us to do, Ruth. We will go with you to the church if you want us to do that and arrange services with the Pastor." Ted stood by nodding his head, too full of sorrow to utter even one word. Marie and John promised Ruth and Ted they would accompany them to the church in the afternoon. The funeral would have to be the next day. "John Mullryne is amassing a cemetery on his plantation. There is a hospital now on the plantation also. Would you like to bury him there? I know there are French soldiers buried there and I could go with you to make the arrangements," John said as he clasped Ted's hand. "You know you are our dearest friends. We have so many memories of our life here with you."

Ted nodded his head. Ruth agreed it was the only thing they could do. There was no way to ship him to England for burial. It would have to be here. It wouldn't be too bad if the British could hold this city. If all the colonies wanted freedom from England it was highly unlikely Georgia would be any different. She wished they had gone to Canada before but now it was too late. Marie and John walked with their friends to the door and promised to be with them in the afternoon.

Johanna was crying silently as she grieved for Gilbert. The last time they saw him he was anxious to get this war over and head back to England. As he went to school there he had encountered a lot of friends. He felt it was an honor to serve with the British military and wanted to make that his career. How dreadful so many lives lost for this war. Johanna hoped Daniel was well. She hoped she wouldn't be required to wait too long until she saw him again. She loved him so much.

They all heard the horses and wagon stop in front of their house. George tied the horses to the rail and helped his family from the wagon. Everyone was glad he was able to enter the city. When asked, George said he had to pay the guards but he was ready to do that. He was desperate to see how they all came through the siege. Mary, Anne, Marian, Virginia and Joshua all came into the house. They all rejoiced to see each other. "We heard all the noise of the artillery even out as far as we were from Savannah," Mary said. Marie hugged all the children and Mary, also George. She was so happy they weren't hurt. She didn't say anything about Gilbert. She thought she would wait until everyone came in. Becky and Wesley came in with Pricella, James, David and Emily. Rachel came in with Kathleen. They were all here. John looked at them all with love in his eyes.

"It gives my heart joy to see you all here with us. God is good. His mercy endureth forever. We must not forget the loss of so many lives as the Colonial army tried to free us from Great Britain. It grieves me to tell you that we have lost a friend in the battle. Gilbert gave his life for what he believed would be the best for us here in Savannah. I will be making the coffin and we will be going to the church this afternoon to make arrangements for the funeral with Rev. Roberts. There will be no gifts exchanged for this occasion and the neighbors will be providing the food for the funeral dinner. We will tell you the arrangements when we return this afternoon.'

George was shocked that they lost Ted and Ruth's son. They all knew of his faith and that they would see him again in heaven. George knew Papa would carve an image on the coffin that would indicate his home going to heaven. "He will be buried at the beautiful plantation of Bonaventure, George," John said. "You can help me with the coffin. I need to choose just the right material."

"I will help you with the coffin, Papa. Gilbert went through so much taken as a prisoner. I will go back home alone this afternoon. I hope I can return for the funeral but you know how that is. You never know if they will let me in or not. I guess it will just depend on what is happened while I am gone and then it goes better if the guards know me. I need to go back to feed the stock we have."

John was ready to start on the carpentry work of the coffin. "I know you would have to go back, son. I know Ruth and Ted would understand if you could not return for the funeral." They were soon working away on the project of the coffin. John used his best lumber. He carved a face on the top of the casket and put an arch over the image indicating that Gilbert had passed from life into heaven. The words, "Death is a passageway to eternal life with Jesus," was carved into the wood.

The ladies were busy with plans for the funeral dinner. They knew how much Ted and Ruth were loved by the entire community and they would be there tomorrow to show their sorrow and love for them in their great loss. The young people were playing quiet games. Even the youngest could feel something very terrific had happened. Mary and Rebecca made up the lunch and everyone had just finished it when Ruth and Ted were by to go to the church with Marie and John.

Ruth's eyes were red and swollen. Ted seemed to be in a daze. They walked over to the church. Hardly anyone was on the streets either walking or riding their horses except the British soldiers walking their beat. Rev. Roberts talked to Ruth and Ted about the funeral. One of the British Captains came over to their home that morning and offered to escort the funeral party to the funeral. He would have a military funeral. The men would walk behind the wagon with the casket and the Union Jack would fly in the front of the procession showing that he gave his life for his country of Great Britain. Their Pastor would cooperate with the Chaplain and they would all do as much for the grieving parents as they could.

As they walked back home Marie held Ruth's hand and the men walked behind them in silence. There was nothing more to say. There were British soldiers at the home of Ruth and Ted but they expressed their sympathy and told Ruth to rest and they would fend for themselves to find something to eat. Marie told Ruth she would bring something over for Ruth and Ted. "I don't feel like eating ever again, Marie," Ruth said. "Ted needs to keep up his strength so we would appreciate it for him."

"Ruth, it is too soon to talk to you about this but we pray God will give you strength to get through these few days and to do that you must eat something. I imagine the girls have some kind of soup simmering at the fireplace right now and you must eat at least some of it"

Marie and John went home. George had worked on the coffin while they were gone and as far as he could see it was done. He had to see what Papa thought of it.

John went right out to see what George had accomplished. He knew he was quickly learning the carpenter trade. John was very pleased with the way George had finished the coffin. "It seems you will be able to carry on with the carpenter trade, George. I am very proud of you."

George was putting the tools away. "I was very glad to do it, Papa. Aunt Ruth has always been so kind to us. I guess we saw more of her in the winter when Ted and Gilbert would go off to school in England. They both always welcomed us into their home. I see the British Military make themselves at home in their house. I guess Ted is pleased with that but I doubt if Aunt Ruth likes it. Of course she would never go against Ted's plans."

John was helping put all the scraps of wood away and clearing off his work bench. "Maybe you can help me carry the coffin over to Ted and Ruth's home. They will keep it closed but want the casket holding the body in their front room."

"I'll do that, Papa and then I will head out to the plantation. As I said, I don't know if I will make it back tomorrow or not. Maybe if I tell them it is a Loyalist funeral they will let me come back in."

"Ruth and Ted will understand. Let's get this over there so they can make their plans." They lifted the casket and brought it over to the front door of their friend's house.

Ted heard them before they had a chance to knock on the door. He helped them put it in place near the outer wall. Without saying anything, John and George left the home.

George adjusted the horse's reins and proceeded home. Mary decided to stay with Marie and John overnight. Anne went to her girlfriend, Greta's home. Marian and Virginia went with Johanna and Joshua went with Rachel. George was not stopped as he rode through the entrance of Savannah. Everyone spent a restless night and knew the funeral of tomorrow would be hard to get through.

George returned the next day with a passenger. Young Ted had turned up at the plantation and he was coming to his brother's funeral. He was dressed in his red coat uniform and would easily get through the guards. He had found out about Gilbert the night before when he didn't turn up in camp. He was devastated with the news. He didn't know how his mother and father would cope with this day of burial for their son. He needed to be with them.

The coffin was brought to the church around noon. A group of British soldiers marched beside the casket. The Chaplain walked with them and would discuss with Rev. Roberts the way the service would be conducted. They marched the coffin to the front of the church and then the British soldiers went outside to stand in honor of their comrade. So many other young men lost their lives in this battle but were buried on land round about that was available for this event. The Chaplain tried to attend all the graveside services of the British army. The funeral would be at 2 o'clock that afternoon.

Ruth and Ted were sitting quietly in their home when young Ted came walking in. He ran to his parents putting his arms around both of them. "I couldn't save him, Mother. I was not with him at the time but I was with another squadron. We always meet in the evening unless we are needed for night guard but he didn't make it to our camp outside Savannah. I asked around and found out he had been killed and one of his friends had pulled his body out of the way into the woods. He went with me to find him and we brought him in and reported his death. I guess you know the rest. Oh, Papa, I shall miss him so much," he sobbed. "We usually worked together. How I wish we had been put in the same group."

Ruth and Ted were so glad that Ted lived through the fighting. "We are going over to the church for the funeral, Ted." Ruth said. "All our friends will be there. The British Military will honor him for his service in his home country. May God see fit to end this war so that no one else will be going through what we are doing now."

It was soon time to go over to the church. Ted looked very professional in his uniform, also a very sad young man. They walked into the church and already there were a group of people there waiting for the service. They were a mixture of Loyalists, Patriots, Indians and those who were taking no sides in this war. Ted walked up with his parents to the casket. It gave Ruth comfort to see the carving John had made on the top of the casket indicating they would see Gilbert again. This was not the end. The archway showed he had left this world and entered eternal life with his Savior. Ted and his father could barely see the casket through their tears. Four soldiers stood two on each side of the casket. He would be buried with honors. Charles an Alice came in from Trenches Island and walked up to Gilbert's family. "We are so sorry, Ruth and Ted," Alice said with her handkerchief folded up in her hand and wet with her tears. "We came right away when we heard." Charles stood taller than any one else there and silently shook Ruth, Ted and young Ted's hand. They went to sit beside Marie and John. Star came in next with her husband, Bright Arrow. Ruth was so dear to Star. Their memories went way back to when Ruth and Ted first landed on Georgia land. Star's tribe greeted them all with food and concern for their welfare. Their neighbors, Louise Peach, Peggy and Frank from the tavern came in to express their sympathy. They all sat down as Chaplain and Rev. Roberts came to the front for the funeral service. Everyone was comforted by the service and the casket was set into the wagon bed which would bring him to the burial ground. The women all stayed behind while the men walked with the casket to the graveside.

So many women brought food so it was all set out at the home of Marie and John. They sat down in groups away from the table talking quietly until the men came back. Some of the military had become good friends with Ted and Ruth so they joined the group at the graveside and came back with them to have dinner. After it was over everyone dispersed to their homes. It was an exhausting day to everyone both mentally and physically. They were all brought to wonder about their own life and their place in eternity. Rev. Roberts had a lot of questions to answer in the coming weeks.

"I have been assigned here in the city," young Ted said as he talked to his parents after the funeral. "I guess it will be until the end of the year. It will give me time to regain my strength and be ready to continue with my life. How I hated to leave Gilbert out in the little cemetery. It just breaks my heart." Ted sat down with his head in this hands. Ruth prayed that God would comfort Ted and bring him in a better relationship with his Lord and Saviour.

It was soon time for Christmas. Marie asked Ruth and Ted to celebrate a quiet Christmas with them. George didn't plan on coming into the city. Johanna and Rachel decided to go to their parents. Johanna had only her father so she would do the cooking for their family. Rebecca and Wesley would go to his family. Regardless Marie decided to put a Christmas tree up and to go to church with Ted and Ruth this Christmas Eve.

As they went to church that evening they passed the Lower New Square where on August 10, 1776 the Declaration of Independence was first read to Georgians inside the colonial Council House. "Remember, Ruth, when we were there to hear it read and the Stars and Stripes were flying high that day." Ted was talking to John and didn't hear her remark. "May it please God that the Stars and Stripes will go up and the Union Jack will be torn down." Ruth nodded in assent, just wishing for an end to this war.

Little did they know that God would answer their prayer and in four years the Stars and Strips would be flying over the city and the Union Jack would come down.

www.ingramcontent.com/pod-product-compliance
Lightning Source LLC
LaVergne TN
LVHW050234220925
821650LV00006B/72